The Art of Losing

The Art of Losing

Paul Williams

Bridge House

British Library Cataloguing in Publication Data
A Record of this Publication is available from the British
Library

ISBN 978-1-907335-61-7

This edition published 2019 by Bridge House Publishing
Manchester, England

All Bridge House books are published on paper derived
from sustainable resources.

So many things seem filled with the intent to be lost

Elizabeth Bishop, One Art

Contents

Introduction

These are stories I have gathered from my experience of living on five continents, of living through war, dictatorships, a religious cult, working with refugees, of losing houses, countries, people and identities.

J.M. Coetzee claims that 'all autobiography is storytelling; all writing is autobiography'. The interesting thing about writing these short stories – and you will know this if you have ever grappled with transmuting real life experience into fiction, or discovered that your fiction is more autobiographical than you first thought – is that the story form itself dictates the trajectory of the story. I have tried to follow the truth of the events I describe (down to the details of the glint of sun on the fender of the Volvo that the Iraqi man is washing an hour before his daughter is killed by a roadside bomb), but I have had to also follow the truth that emerges when writing a story, a deeper truth in a language I am only beginning to understand. A narrative may begin with an idea, an image, an intent or a slice of lived experience, but the act of telling transforms it into something else – art. And by art I do not mean 'Art' with a capital A, but the skill of crafting, words. The art of losing is also a skill one acquires through failure, betrayal, heartache.

Most of these stories have been published in various literary journals around the world over many years, but as I gather them together, I find that they have common themes, strands that twine through them – survival, slivers of glass or debris embedded in skin, the weight of relationships, and loss. Losing things is the quintessential human experience.

Elizabeth Bishop's poem 'One Art' (1979) was initially called 'The Art of Losing'. On the surface, the poem is about how easy it is to acquire the skill of losing things. Start small, with keys, then move onto houses, continents, people. But she is being ironic – at a deeper level she is struggling with the pain of loss. '*Write* it!' she says in the last line, and so transforms loss into art where writing about loss allows the author to regain something, 'unlose' it.

After I wrote my memoir *Soldier Blue* (2008) about growing up in a civil war, for example, the PSTD and nightmares ceased. The past transformed through art into a thing of value, not a regret or a wound – but an artefact: art as scar tissue, perhaps.

These twenty stories lurch from continent to continent, from child to teen to adult, from past to present, from war to peace, from me to you. Please accept my gift of loss, transformed by art.

Paul Williams
Weyba Downs, Australia
2019

Happy Birthday Frank

He arrived at five on a Sunday morning. Haggard from the long haul flight from Brisbane, he stumbled through the mazes of the underground, dragged his suitcase with the broken handle along interminable tunnels of concrete. The last thing he expected at the bottom of a long escalator at Victoria Station was a knot of men and women at the tail end of an all-night party. Each carried a pink and silver heart-shaped balloon. He tried to slide past but a man handed him a balloon, with HAPPY BIRTHDAY FRANK printed on one side.

'Who's Frank?' he asked.

'You are. Happy birthday, Frank.'

He held the balloon tight, and it pulled against him in the draught of the arched ceiling.

On the Northern Line to Tooting Bec, he gripped the balloon's pink string with one hand and hugged the suitcase with the other. The balloon bobbed against the roof of the carriage.

The Tube had its rules: no one smile, no one make eye contact, no one intrude into personal space, even if your nose is in their armpit. Fortunately a December Sunday morning meant room for all. The passengers sat in a row opposite him, and rocked themselves to sleep to the rhythm of the train. Some read *The Metro*, the free newspaper that littered the carriage. Some stared past him through the window at the passing stations, their pupils dancing left and right as if they were having a *petit mal* fit. A woman directly opposite him in tight black clothes (nothing unusual – everyone wore black) looked up at the balloon and then down at him. Smiled. Closed her eyes.

She had a mouth like a shrew, wore black eyeliner and mauve lipstick, displayed glitter black fingernails, and sported a short black dress. Tight black stockings emerged from tight black knee high boots. She had dressed up for the ride. A Tube Rider. She looked older than he, in her late twenties, at least. Her skin revealed her Englishness – that is to say, underbelly toad white and unblemished by sun or wrinkles.

She opened her eyes. He stared at the Tube map above her head, counting how many stops he had to go. 22. 21. 20.

But her eyes focused on the balloon. She mouthed the words, Happy Birthday Frank. He adjusted his suitcase and transferred the balloon to his left hand.

At her station, Clapham South, she stood, held the strap above his seat and lurched toward him as the train screeched to a grinding stop. She leaned over him and mouthed the words again, this time aloud: 'Happy Birthday Frank.' He stared at her shoulders and hair as she stepped out of the train and past his window. Their eyes met. He waved. She waved back with two fingers and turned the corner.

The deal was this: he was to inhabit the flat in Tooting Bec for a week of London culture and adventure; his cousin would take his cottage in Northern New South Wales for a week of summer by the Pacific Ocean.

His cousin had the better end of the deal by far. The subterranean London flat reeked of mould. Once the four storey building had been a Victorian mansion, he guessed, but had since been divided into four vertical apartments, and the old servants' quarters below the level of the street had been converted into a granny flat. His ceiling was so low, he could flatten his palm against it when he stood, and all evening, neighbours creaked like elephants above him. This flat could fit into his modest living room at home. Nevertheless, this was London, the flat within walking distance to a Tube stop, and he could have – as his brother said – an adventure.

Life. Experience The Big City. The people. Maybe you'll meet someone. And don't forget to bolt and latch the front door every time.

He let the balloon go at last. It rose slowly to the ceiling, and hid in the corner of the room, its string dangling on the couch.

He was not interested in buildings and shows and history. People fascinated him. And the best place to see people was on the Tube. He had bought a week travel card (Off Peak), and planned to spend most of his days underground.

He hoped to bump into the woman he had encountered on that first Tube ride from the airport. Fat chance of that. How many millions of people traversed this city every day? He saw many doubles, triples, quadruples of her, of course – women in tight black skirts, black stockings, boots, and tight mouths. But not her.

He gave her a name – Emily. She looked like an Emily. He took it from the Simon and Garfunkel CD he found in his cousin's CD collection. For Emily wherever I may find her – a fragment of a song, a haunting dream, and images of hair on a pillow, dark alleyways, church bells ringing.

Happy Birthday Frank. The way her eyes smiled. The way she spoke, in a husky collusive whisper. The way she turned her head, as if in slow motion, and the wave – two fingers, signifying something. Her face, her smile, her gestures burned into the retina of his memory, and, surprisingly, into his heart. He played that brief scenario over and over in his mind. In his dreams, he felt the shadow of her face over him as she bent down, he felt her hair tickle his face, and he felt her kiss. He could even hear her voice, husky, low. Happy Birthday Frank. But he woke up cold and bereft.

What if he had run after her that day, followed her? Excuse me...? Lumbering with his suitcase. She would have turned, smiled... and...

He explored Hampton Court maze, the Tower of London and the Houses of Parliament. He waded through tourists the way he swished through the sugarcane plantation at home. The world rolled on and off at every Tube stop. Weary travellers from Heathrow clung to labelled suitcases that told everyone exactly where they came from and where they were going. He recognised Aussies too, and he slid back, hoping not to be recognised as one of them.

He lurked at the Clapham South Tube station, walked its streets. Finally, he placed an ad in *The Metro*. Foolish. Silly. But worth a shot.

'Emily'... we met on the Northern Line Sunday, 23rd October, 8 a.m. I had the Happy Birthday Frank balloon. Please contact me at this number. 'Frank.'

He watched women on the Tube flicking impatiently past his ad, moving their eyes quickly over it. Somewhere on the Tube, she would read it.

His clothes grew grimy. London was, he decided, black. So he bought black Levi jeans, a black Levi shirt, black Doc Marten boots and a black trench coat he found second-hand in Camden market. His skin felt pallid. Petal-like. He developed black rings under his eyes.

He watched people, guessed the story of their lives, where they were going, what their names were, their occupations. Outside the station, groups of women talked loudly, swore, laughed, accosted him. 'Going the wrong way?' they cat-called as he passed late Tuesday night. 'You need to come with us!'

The thing to do of course was to replicate that Sunday journey. At that precise time and place. But this was impossible. Next Sunday he would be returning to Heathrow, and home.

On Wednesday, he visited Trafalgar Square, Covent Garden, Piccadilly, St John's, Big Ben, the Wheel, and between each, sat in the Tube, watched people. Lurked at Clapham South.

On Thursday, he played with the temptation to take his balloon back with him on the train – it was still semi-buoyant, thudding against the ceiling of the room, but had now found an air vent which it kept playing with, returning to and racing away from. Perhaps the balloon would find her. Or it would at least single him out as the boy with the balloon. Perhaps raise a smile in this mass of unsmiling humanity.

But he didn't need to stand out even more. He already stood out. Something about his face. Perhaps he still looked too much at other people, caught their eyes, something you mustn't do here. He was too curious perhaps, not aloof enough. He rode the Tube as an end in itself, and it showed. He wasn't going anywhere, as all these people were.

Friday evening, he walked through Soho. A passing white haired man felt him up, women in glass cubicles where neon lights flashed the word GIRLS over and over again harangued him, and he returned dejected to the Tube.

But at Clapham South, a woman at the far end of the carriage, her back to him, behind a thick crowd of standing passengers shouldered her way off the train.

Emily. The same skirt, hair, top, boots.

He squeezed his way out the train entrance to watch her step over the gap and into the lava flow of people upstairs. He pushed past people – bad decorum in these parts: you have to be patient, wait your turn, shuffle behind the crowd. 'Excuse me… I just have to… please… Sorry.'

Outside the station, the air blew white and the

pavements black. Which way did she go? He heard the clicking of heels. In London, women walked alone at night, unafraid. He picked out against the streetlight a dark shape – black clothes, black hair – clicking heels up the street. He followed. She walked faster, as if she sensed he was stalking her; he matched her pace. She did not turn. Wet pavements reflected the neon lights of the fish and chip shop and taxi rank, and as he splashed through the puddles, the reflection shattered into a kaleidoscope of weak colours.

She turned into an alleyway. A dark figure turning a key in a door. She looked up, and in the glint of the reflected neon light, he saw a stranger. Not her. He saw panic in her white hands as she turned the key, pushed open the door and slid in. The door slammed. Latched. Bolted.

Sorry, sorry, he said to the cold air, his breath a dragon's hiss of steam.

The flat echoed with his despair as he unlocked, unlatched, turned the dead bolt home. Happy Birthday Frank! The balloon stirred in the gust of wind as the heat came on, looked sadder and sadder, but still floated.

On the last night – Saturday – he resigned himself to the fact that the one brief moment – how long was it – ten or twenty seconds? – was all he would have of her. His whole life he would remember that moment. And she would never know.

Obsession grows from the smallest seeds. She had gouged an ache in his soul, big enough for a lost continent, a lost world, a lost childhood.

Maybe she too replayed that moment in her mind: the boy with the balloon – what was his name? Frank. Happy Birthday Frank, why didn't I beckon him, invite him home? But more likely, this incident in her hard drive was immediately sent to the trash.

Saturday night on the train from London Victoria, at around midnight, a woman sat down opposite him. A woman in a black pencil skirt. Thirty maybe. Same clothes, boots, mascara. Smiling hard at him, unashamedly staring, three feet away, her body jiggling to the bumping and scraping of the train.

But not her. Not Emily.

He avoided her eye.

No chance. One furtive glance at her was all it took: she stood up, staggered across to him, and slumped onto the vacant seat on his left. 'God, you're beautiful,' she said.

She must be very, very drunk, he thought. She leaned hard against him, pinning his arm to the armrest.

He feigned a smile at the other passengers – in apology – but being British, they didn't give anything away. Not even a smile or twitch of the eye. The man opposite read *The Metro*. The woman on his right stared ahead into some other world far away. The teenagers behind him were attached by wires to devices that went tak tak tak ccchhh, tak tak tak ccchhh.

She placed her left hand on his black Levi's, a white, white hand with a wedding ring wedged on her ring finger.

'What's your name?' It took her whole face to say the words.

'Frank.'

'Frank? Listen, honey, I'm too drunk to drive. Can you drive me home?'

She fumbled in the top pocket of her waistcoat. Underneath she wore a skimpy tank top, and little else. In winter, in London. Apparently British women didn't feel the cold.

He recoiled from her garlic beer breath, from her invasion of his personal space. One thing to fantasise; another for a shy boy to respond as he did in dreams. Besides, he wanted *her*. 'Drive? We're on a train.'

She dangled the keys. 'See.' Placed them in the palm of his hand and closed his fist over them. 'Don't lose them, for God's sake.'

Clapham South. Balham. Tooting Bec. The doors banged open. He disentangled himself. Stood. 'It's my stop. I have to go.' He held out her keys.

'Mine too. This is my stop.' She clung to him as he tried to escape, and held his trench coat by the lapels as he sidled past the other passengers. 'Come on,' she said. 'We have to hurry.'

She fell, because he had dragged her along in his bid to get away. 'Sorry.'

He picked her up, surprised at how heavy she was, this slim waif. He hoisted her over the gap between the platform and the train. He placed her down on the ground on her feet, but they gave way under her. She leaned on him and he had to half carry her out of the station and into the car park. She was right – she'd had way too much to drink. Too drunk to drive. 'So where's your car?'

She looked bewildered. 'Was this my stop?'

All station platforms looked the same to him: the same low seedy humming depression, the small mean car parks, the lack of warm shelter from the wind. Only the names – the absurd names – distinguished them.

'I parked it here, I swear.' Her eyes were wide. 'Do you think it's been stolen?'

In the dark, he saw Emily: prim mouth, black hair, black stockings, black short dress, black way-too-small top. Even a belly-ring – something he had missed before. 'Sure this is your station?'

'Tooting Bec? No. We were on the Victoria Line, right?'

'Northern. It's my station.'

'Christ.'

He sighed. 'It's a two minute walk to my place.'

He helped her up the gleaming street, as best as he could. She leaned heavily on him, stumbled, made him weave. Her breath streamed white in the amber light of the street signs. Her face felt ice cold as she pressed against his neck.

'You sure you don't want me to take you home? I can still take you home. Where do you live?'

She looked confused. 'Can't I stay at your place? Promise I won't take up space. Just a sofa in your living room.'

He thought: some men prowl the Tube for years looking for drunk women to pick up and take home.

'Are you cold? You want my coat?'

'Where the hell do you come from?'

He did not know how to answer the question. 'Australia.'

This was funny, apparently. 'Australia?' She accented the first syllable, then the second, then the third, then the fourth. He could see the image the word evoked in her mind, but did not correct it.

'Here we are.'

He fumbled with the key, pushed open the vault of his flat.

'Your name *is* Frank. I thought you were bullshitting me. No one has a name like Frank.'

She pulled the pink string and the balloon curtseyed down and up, then slowly thudded its way back to its corner.

'You should let it go, you know. It can't survive here.'

He stared up at the sagging balloon.

'It's going to die in here. You have to let it out.'

'It's done pretty well – a week and it's still floating.'

'Barely.'

And with that she slumped onto the couch and passed

out. He covered her with a blanket, placed a pillow under her head, watched her for a while, then went to bed.

Emily hovered above him, whispering. The balloon thudded every so often when the heating came on and off.

And in the morning, he could not find her. Empty couch bathroom, and wallet. His credit cards and money had been taken, of course, though she had kindly left his passport, air ticket and Travel Pass. She also left a rumpled blanket and a long strand of black hair on a dented pillow. A note scrawled on the telephone pad read: Happy Birthday Frank!

He locked the door for the last time and rolled his suitcase on its plastic wheels along the cracked pavement. In his free hand, he held a pink and white balloon, still half buoyant. At the entrance to the Tube station, he looked up at the sky. He took his last breath of white air before climbing into a metal tube carriage, imagined the metal moving passageway at Heathrow, and finally the metal tube of the A380 to Singapore and Brisbane. A luminous hope still beat in his chest: he would see her on the Tube to Heathrow, by some fortuitous synchronicity.

He believed in symmetry, even though so far his life had shown him only disproportioned fractals.

His fingers numbed in the wind.

Commuters jostled him, unseeing, lowering their dead-pan faces as he held a sagging heart-shaped silver and pink balloon with the words Happy Birthday Frank on it.

He let it go. Unsure of its new-found freedom, the balloon hovered for a moment, and then stuttered up to the chimney rooftops of the terraced housing lining the street. He watched it trip and then find its way above the rooftops. In the grey morning of a new foggy London day, he watched it bob and duck and rise until it became a speck. He willed it to fly higher.

The Art of Losing

He heard it first, a curious rushing noise. Stopped to listen. Then he saw – he ran for his Ute, fumbled with the keys, but before he could open the door, a wall of water two metres high smashed into it. He scrambled onto the bonnet, clung to the roof rack. The surge of muddy water rocked the car, as if testing its weight, and then – incredibly – lifted the car and slammed it into the wall of his house. He clung on, but then spied the drainpipe and leaped for it, climbed up onto the slate roof. A wall of red-brown water battered the side of the house, smashed through the screened veranda below him, and stormed inside. The Ute slammed against the wall again and again, before being sucked around the house towards what used to be a gully, now a foamy brown torrent.

He watched this brown serpent suck everything into its vortex. It filled the cattle dip, buckled and dragged it to the lower river. A tree, roots up, raced past, and then he recognised (or thought he recognised) his grove of olive tree saplings dancing down the current.

The level of water – no, not water, brown mud, sticks, debris – rose higher up the wall of the house. He straddled the apex of the roof, pulled out his mobile phone, held it as steady as he could, and dialled 000.

No reception, of course. Never good reception down in the valley at the best of times. He slid it back into his pocket.

He picked out the debris of a neighbour's house – the whole living room wall, a lounge suite, a metal gate, tangled barbed wire. And following laboriously behind, clunking on the shallow ground, a Winnebago caravan. It lurched close to the house, snagged on a submerged clothesline, he guessed from its position, whumped past him, hit the side of the house and then stuck fast in the top branches of his Moreton Fig.

His horses?

He turned to the east, but instead of his paddocks he saw a brown undulating stew punctuated with bleeding tree branches.

A passing parade of death.

Another Ute (his neighbour's?) floated by, thudding on what had recently been his tennis court, the light poles still steadfastly erect.

After an hour, it rose no higher. Just below the eaves, brown sludge bubbled and slushed. Beneath him, the weight of it had smashed the French door and poured through into the living room. His house offered no more resistance; it had given up trying. How many hours did he wait up there? He didn't know. He shivered violently, his boots sticky and heavy with mud. He had wedged his back against the chimney to rest, and his legs gripped the tiles.

And then the mobile phone in his pocket rang.

'David?' His wife.

'Marge. Marge.'

She was on top of the range, in Toowoomba, safe, at work.

'David,' she said. 'You won't believe what's happening up here. The town's in flood. A wall of water... Good job you stayed home today. I barely missed it all down Russell. Can you believe it?'

'Marge...?'

'Don't come into work today. They've closed the uni anyway... and the roads are gone.'

'The roads?'

'Murphy's creek. The range is still open... I think... David, you still there?'

'Yes.'

'Car park flooded, office... David? You OK?'

21

'It's under water.' He swept his arm at the brown around him where the farm had been.

'What?'

'Everything. The house... and the whole of Murphy's Creek. Gone. I mean the creek is everywhere.'

'David...?' A pause. 'Where are you?'

The helicopter rescue he could only recall afterwards through other people's eyes. He saw it on TV, aerial shots of others being rescued from rooftops, swinging up on wires. He saw himself in the third person. Grateful because so many had been washed away in their vehicles.

He and Marge stayed with his brother, the one he hadn't been on speaking terms with for years. But the flood washed away many things. And brought new things: a tiny bedroom; his brother's pyjamas, clothes, his brother's hospitality. They skirted around the knots of the awkward past like slow brown serpents.

Until then, he hadn't lost anything. It was all sub-aqua. 'When it recedes,' his brother said, 'we'll go and see what's there. What's left.'

That first night in his brother's house, the images swirled past him. In his nightmares, he waded thickly in the mud through the past inventory of his possessions, dragging them up into his waking starts. Waiting for the flood to recede in his mind.

Inventory of lost items:

Ties

Grandfather's button accordion, never played,
    brought across from Ireland in 1900

China set

Set of tools

His wife woke him up after midnight. 'What happened to the horses?'

'I don't think they survived.'

In the morning, on TV, they saw horses with nostrils flared, swimming in Brisbane floodwaters, clambering on rooftops, perched with cows, like so many magpies. A man up a tree with a snake.

'I feel sorry for the animals,' she said. 'They don't know what's going on.'

'Marge, for Christ's sake.'

Over the next few days, everything emerged from the floodwaters of his mind. What they had lost. Were losing. Would still lose. These things bobbed up and down, knocking him awake, insisting on their existence. He got up, wrote in the dark.

'What are you doing?'

'The list. For insurance purposes.'

The ride-on mower.

The insurance documents.

The Persian rug.

Pride. Dignity. Independence. Sovereignty. The Past. The Future.

The briefcase with their passports and documents. The computer with all its files. The photo albums. The tax papers. The hard drive. The jewellery. The slow-cooker.

'The horses,' she said. 'Did you see the animals on TV with their wild eyes? And that family clinging to a Ute going down the river?'

'For Christ's sake, Marge. Stop crying, will you?'

The Lockyer valley had disappeared. A disaster zone, important enough for politicians to fly over in helicopters and give speeches about.

'I'm going back.'

'You can't,' she said. 'It's closed. See, road closed. Postman's Ridge washed away, the bridges gone.'

'I'm going back,' he said.

'They won't let you.'

'Won't let me go to my own house?'

'The roads are gone. The bridge's gone. It's dangerous.'

Meanwhile, the lost items multiplied. What about the books he had borrowed from Jack last week? The certificates on the walls of his study? The things in his dreams were mischievous – they slipped like Mercury through his fingers.

Marge hadn't stopped crying. A flood of tears, that's what it was, he reasoned to himself. A cleaning out, a mechanism of the body to flush out all grief, all impurities. He was dry and irritable. A stone. But he had always been a stone.

Material assistance came swiftly, or rather, the promise of assistance came swiftly. He would be compensated with cash to start, to get back on his feet, and then the insurance would kick in.

David taught English language to Sudanese, Congolese and Somali refugees. 'I've lost everything,' he told his students, when he returned to work a week later. 'Everything.' The irony didn't escape him. He had taken this job to help those who had lost everything – their childhoods, countries, dignity, and language.

'A work party has been organised for Saturday morning,' said his boss. 'A group of us got together and decided to head out to your property and see what we can do.'

He shook his head. 'I'm OK.'

'You don't have to come if you don't want. We can sort everything out. Clean up the mess.'

'I want to be there.'

The water had receded leaving the farm submerged in

brown sludge. The outside walls of the house were coated mud-brown up to the eaves. He couldn't even get in the door. The contents of the house has been flushed through the corridors and outside at the back, unrecognisable brown statues in a foreign landscape. Through the French doors, the sludge had buried the living room to the ceiling, but had now receded to two feet. The light fittings were tangled in barbed wire and tree branches. A sideboard which had contained delicate china plates lay on its back, the china plates gone. But a bookshelf stood stubbornly against the back wall and an entire shelf of Encyclopaedia Britannica remained intact.

In the back yard, he saw the cattle dip, a mangled toy in the scrub by the river; his Ute? Gone. The neighbour's caravan lodged high in the tree. Fences, gone. Tennis court, ripped up; orchard trees, swept away. Nothing left. Nothing to salvage. He checked stinking ditches and ravines.

He had come with a pen and paper to make an inventory of all damaged items, of all things saved, to match them to his imaginary list. But he never took the pen and paper out of his jacket pocket.

Dozens of helpers picked their way through the rubble. Fifty people, he counted. A contingent of Sudanese men, with cheerful dispositions. Patatrick, the Congolese student who had grown up in a refugee camp, had been coerced into becoming a child soldier, fighting an unspeakable war rummaged in the brown soup and pulled out unrecognisable shapes. A phalanx of sun-damaged Zimbabweans, ex-farmers themselves, whose land had been seized by Robert Mugabe's war veterans, swept through the killing ground in a long line.

By the end of the day, the volunteers had sorted the debris into piles as high as the water that had brought them there. The hardy Zimbabweans wrestled together with frail

Somali men to pull the cattle grid out of the ditch; shovels scraped and piled up the mud from the house into slag heaps on what had once been the front lawn. Children combed the fields for belongings, running in triumph with articles and bric-a-brac.

A Sudanese man debated with him as to whether to bring the caravan down from the big tree. In the end, they decided against it. 'It belongs to my neighbour,' said David. 'He was planning a grey tour this year. He put his entire pension into buying it. Better leave it there.'

The ornaments on the top shelf of the kitchen and a few never-used appliances remained untouched. The Encyclopaedia Britannica volumes pulled out of the bookcase stayed intact, their pages tightly crisp and white. The Sudanese man presented these saved items to him as an offering.

He found no briefcase, no tax files, no photo albums, no precious mementoes in his wife's dressing table drawer – even the dressing table was gone. The few papers splattered against the fence were not his. The contents of an entire house raked up on the back paddock were not his either. Nothing on the list in his mind appeared. As if it never existed, or belonged to another man from another era. A phantom list of an imaginary life he thought he had lived.

'Downstream!' someone called. There they found the horses, grazing on higher ground, whisking their tails. Caked with mud, serene. 'Still feel sorry for them, Marge?'

They drank hot tea at sunset. 'Sorry, David,' said his boss, 'we made piles of rubbish on your property, but not much of it is yours.'

'I have my 1970 Encyclopaedia Britannica and my George Foreman Mean Lean grilling machine. What more do I need?'

'Don't worry, mate, they'll compensate. You'll have it all back. Everything. Back to normal. Insurance companies are paying out fortunes.'

He made many phone calls to tinny voices in Melbourne and Sydney; he filled out complicated claim forms. 'So when do I get compensated?'

A semantic problem arose. For a flood, yes, the insurance company would gladly pay out, but was this technically a flood? 'We have to work out what actually happened,' said the voice on the phone.

'You mean, I pay you premiums all my life, you erect huge glass buildings in Sydney with my money, and then you don't know what a flood is?'

'While you're covered for damage caused by storm, rain or flash flooding, our documents show that you're not insured for flood under the company's definition.'

'We don't need to fight with anyone,' said his wife. 'Don't get upset.'

'I'm not upset,' he said. 'A sense of the ridiculous is medicine to the soul.'

She watched him caress beers with his brother on the veranda each evening. She felt his warm touch at night. Something was happening to him. The stone he had been, that pinched life he had lived had changed. And Marge? Her tears flushed out all sorts of things from her past too. The way they never used to talk, the way they had hardened into a grim routine.

No one had alerted the postie that the house had been abandoned to the elements, or that the farm flailed in mud. Mail kept arriving, the mailbox stuffed, and David had to drive down the range every few days to collect the glossy pizza delivery coupons, gym ads, garden service cards, and bills. He would return to Toowoomba and use them to fuel his brother's barbeque every Saturday evening.

Two months after the flood, he received an electricity bill for three hundred and twenty five dollars and fifty-two cents. He called the number on the bill. 'Why have I received this?'

'Your last two months' electricity usage, sir.'

'How did you get this figure?'

'We read your meter.'

'You personally?'

'No.'

'I defy you to read the electricity meter. In fact, why don't you come up here and read my meter. We'll read it together…'

The electricity meter lay buried deep in dried red mud. No power could possibly connect to the remains of the house.

'I'm in Melbourne, sir.'

'I'm not paying this bill. Ever.'

'Sir, that's not advisable. You could be taken to court.'

'You come up here and take me to court. Make me pay it.'

He had the impunity of the dispossessed. He relished in that freedom. Dispossessed. A good word. He wore these new words like clothes. Everything. Nothing. Compensation. Flood victim. And now Dispossessed.

Every morning, his office at work piled with gifts. Sometimes anonymous, sometimes with notes of condolence. And gifts from the dispossessed themselves, those who had everything taken away. From the Sudanese man, a pen and pencil set. From the Zimbabwean ex-farmers, a gift voucher for Bunnings. We know what it's like, they said with their gifts. And at last, someone else knows what it's like.

Couscous, flavoured with herbs and sympathy from the Libyan women. They knew dispossession too: in 2010, the

Libyan government stopped sending them cheques for student fees and living expenses. Whenever he casually remarked about some item he had lost, there it would appear the next day, as if by magic. Expensive ties, bought by the Congolese students at a price that would have fed their family back home for a week.

Instead of anger and frustration, something barely recognisable replaced the numbness of shock and defeat.

'You're a refugee now sir,' said Patatrick.

'All in the same boat,' he said.

'We never needed all those things,' he told his wife. 'We thought they were our past, our identity, that they held us together.'

'You want to live with your brother forever?'

He considered. 'Our garage was full of rubbish, Marge. Do you want all that stuff back? We have to let it all go.'

'Sometimes I just don't understand you,' she said.

After five months, they had moved into the guest cottage at the back of his brother's property. The insurance company finally phoned with the good news. 'You can rebuild the house.'

'What if we don't want to rebuild? What if we don't want to reproduce our old life?'

'But sir, there's no proviso for...'

'I'm not building there. Wait for the next flood to come along and wipe us out again?'

'The statistics show that it should never happen again in your lifetime...'

'No,' he said. 'I'm not building there. And what's the point of going back to our old life. We don't want it.'

And six months after the flood, an envelope with a key from Mr Anonymous arrived, with a short note. 'You don't know me; I'm on contract in Dubai. I have a house load of brand new furniture and white appliances in a storage facility in Brisbane. It's been sitting there doing nothing for over a year. I don't need it. It's yours. When you have a house, there's a lounge and dining room suite, three beds, fridge, stove, washer, drier. Don't go buying anything before you check your new container.'

'Maybe we can rebuild now,' said his wife that night as they lay together. 'But higher up on the property nearer the post box, on poles. We have everything we need to fill the house.'

Somewhere deep inside him, a warm and unfamiliar freedom stirred. 'We can't go back,' he said. 'Is that a bad thing?'

Stars spread across the sky. Crickets sang in the bushes. She lay quiet for a moment her eyes dry. 'No,' she said. 'No, it's not a bad thing.'

The President

Canst thou, O partial sleep, give thy repose
To the wet sea-boy in an hour so rude,
And in the calmest and most stillest night,
With all appliances and means to boot,
Deny it to a king? Then happy low, lie down!
Uneasy lies the head that wears a crown.

It is the same nightmare over and over again. Strange, it recurs every night, building in more and more detail.

In the dream, he stands on the top of a hill, looking down. All mine, all mine, he says. But the green valley quickly turns into a desert. It begins to writhe with worms. No, they are not worms, they are dead souls, carrying their lifeless forms with them – crushed bones, deformed faces, bloody entrails, and calling out to him, reaching up hands to grab his cloak – yes, he is wearing a strange woman's cloak.

A flood of twenty, thirty, forty thousand people, all dead, all bloody, apparitions rushing at him... All the people he has had killed, in chronological order, when he was commander in chief; first the petty kills when in training, then when he was in power, the Third Brigade purges, the car crashes.

Who are you?

We are the envoys sent by Ndabaningi Sithole to meet you. You ordered us captured, murdered and laid out in a line at the side of the road as a warning to local people.

And you?

Don't you remember the car accidents? Those you ordered killed in car accidents?

I never ordered any...

Border Gezi.

Moven Mahachi.

Elliot Manyika.

Christopher Ushowekunzwe.

Peter Pamire.

And you?

An army of twenty thousand, three hundred and fifty seven chanting men, women and children. Yes, even children. But he doesn't have to ask this time. 'We are the chaff that blew away in the wind. You have heard us calling you night after night from those deep mineshafts.'

'Any more?'

A few stragglers, white farmers, farm labourers. And finally a shadow of a man, limping along, bloody-faced, talking loud above the murmur of the undead, a finger waving in the President's face: 'The dead are always with you,' he said. 'And we keep count.'

'Who are you?'

'You are accountable, for every man and woman and child you have killed. Every hair on their head is numbered.'

'The Rhodesians did this... The British...' The President cries out in his dream, but strangely, his voice is high. 'Cecil Rhodes cut through our land with a broad sword of destruction. He killed our people, brought his never-ending train of robbers and pirates, and Rhodesians, who continued to kill and decimate our people. These are his dead, not mine...'

He is not being heard. The shadow wags its finger. 'And then the judgment. And every deed and thought will be brought forth. We will know, meanwhile we wait, we cry out, we make our supplication known.'

The dream always ends the same way too – a rumble of thunder, a stampede of starving women, skeletons, children with bloated stomachs, hobbling along, millions running at him, stamping bare feet. He feels his own bones crush, his innards squelch out. And then he is falling into a mineshaft of cold dark steel blackness. Falling, falling, falling, falling.

His Excellency, the President of the Republic of Zimbabwe stares out of the window of his living room at his full-length pool. It laps turquoise against the French doors, shimmers like a mirage and mirrors the sky. He has never swum in it. No one as far as he knows has ever swum in it. Yet the gardener religiously cleans it with a large scoop, fishing out leaves and centipedes. The Kreepy-Krawly thuds its way around the bottom sucking up the corpses of Christmas beetles.

The house is marble and stucco, with colonnades, a Louis IXV Versailles planted in sub-tropical Africa. Every window is arched and heavily ornamented with columns, frills, fake coats of arms. And why not? He did not intend his retirement house to look this way – he simply let his wife order from catalogues. Strange, in every other way he is in control of his life, his country, his foreign policy; he held the West at bay by sheer force of his own personality, yet at home, she rules. Or rather, he indulges her.

He watched the boxes arrive, the carpenters and builders hammer and clink away, and at each new addition, his heart sank. 'You're building a Roman villa!' he shouted at the workers who grinned at him and indicated the plans, the instructions, and the woman standing over them.

So he is a stranger in this marble palace, wandering through its hallways, ducking under its heavy chandeliers and passing through its arched and achingly vacuous caverns. And now he is ill, the cancer slowly creeping through his bones.

He has everything his heart desires, he has to tell himself, to fill the emptiness of these chambers. And it does not stop. Today, he spies a pile of new boxes at the door to her room. She is back then from her latest shopping trip in London.

The carpets are plush under his bare feet as he pads to the bathroom. It irks him. He is not a materialist. It means nothing to him. He is happy with simple food, his single bed in the spare room, and his books.

'Comrade President?' He hears the timid knock at the door.

'Have the guests arrived?' he calls out.

'They're all here, sir.'

'I'll be there in moment.'

'This way, your Excellency, your seat at the dinner table is right at the head.'

The president waits for his entourage (the four bodyguards, his attractive child-bride wife) to stand, and then swaggers towards the dinner table. People applaud.

'A traditional feast tonight, Comrade President, *sadza ne mbudzi*.'

Goat, yes, but also pheasant, duck, caviar, prawns from Mozambique, carrots carved in the shape of exotic animals, and a place laid for each of the ten honoured guests. They stand behind their chairs, and servants, one a chair, wait behind them. It is a routine the president is used to. He gives a perfunctory glance at the food, and then at his place.

He starts. He turns in annoyance to the *maitre de*, an over-smiling man. 'But there is no seat for me. Someone has taken my seat.'

'Your Excellency, I can assure you...' The man gestures towards the empty seat. 'The place of Honour as usual.'

But the president blanches. 'Get him out of here! It's him. It's you. Get out of my seat!' His hand trembles. His security men step up and screen him off, and one draws a weapon, a small Luger pistol.

'There's no one there, sir.'

But the president cannot be consoled. 'You can't do this to me!' He staggers back, crashing into the Minister of Education whose stomach cushions the fall. The president cannot take his eyes off the empty chair. 'Why Josiah? Why?'

A murmur rises from the guests. Concerned individuals come to his assistance. The security guard is now examining the table, the chair, the cloth dais behind it, the tent wall. Perhaps his Excellency has spotted a bugging device, or an explosive booby trap. 'Nothing, sir.'

But the President is not listening. 'My god, he's dripping all over the table cloth. Get him away. The food is ruined…'

A wave of sympathetic murmurs fill the tent. 'Josiah!? Whom does he mean?' But they know. It is no secret that he lays a place for Josiah Tongogara at every meal.

He does not hear them. He does not see them. His vision is transfixed by some terror hovering in front of his eyes. 'Why are you showing me this, Josiah?'

'We should have laid a place for his imaginary friend,' whispers the General to the *Maitre De*.

'Can no one stop him?' says the president, with arms outstretched and blind eyes, as if sleepwalking.

A woman screams as he jostles her in his bid to grab whatever imaginary object he sees hovering in the air. The security guards usher people out, screening them away from the swaying president. 'He is unwell,' calls the Minister of Defence. 'Give him air. Let him breathe. Please clear the tent.'

They bolt out of the entrance flap, some looking back to see the President – their President – flaying his arms in terror, swatting imaginary giant bats around his head. 'We are cancelling the banquet. Please leave in an orderly fashion.'

The bath is ready, a stooping servant informs him, so he slips into the one room that embarrasses him most of all. Its white tiles and mirrored walls make it look like a sacrificial altar, with its raised Jacuzzi and four columns. He drops his ill-fitting clothes, and steps in. The servant has got the temperature just right this time. He sinks into the foam, finds the seat ledge where he can lie and stare out of the window at the tall fir trees in a line at the back of the house. Not that he feels dirty; he feels too clean. His life is like a sterilised hospital and he is in quarantine.

He lies back in the bath and closes his eyes, always a dangerous thing.

He stiffens. The breeze blowing through a closed and locked window tells him that he is not alone.

He opens his eyes. 'Who's there?'

Nothing. He emerges from the bath and stands before the full-length mirror, scrutinises his reflection. What does he see? A sad figure, shrunken and withered, in spite of the Botox injections. His hair needs dying again. Without his glasses, the world is a blur. He used to see an image of his ideal self; he used to see the picture on the campaign t-shirts, on the election posters. But now he just looks old.

He can feel the dead watching him, even now. He can no longer keep the voices quiet. Even the drugs, the pitter-patter of applause everywhere he goes is not enough.

He jumps. A sepia skinned man stands before him. Short stubbly hair, stubbly unshaven face, dressed exactly the way he was on the day he was killed. Wearing the Chinese uniform he sported as a general. And in the reflection of the mirror, he stares with accusing eyes.

'Josiah? What do you want?'

The man speaks. 'When did you betray this country? Was it in 1979 just before you took power? Or was it in 1982? 1985? 1990? Again and again, over and over, the dead have been showing up at my door, complaining about you. All those car accidents, Robert. Why? What about the revolution? The dreams we talked about of this country... What we fought for all those years?'

The President turns away, but the man steps through the glass and into the room. 'Tell me, Robert, tell me then what you have done for this country?'

The President burbles. 'You know what I have done. The revolution is complete. I have done all I have promised.'

The man shakes his head. 'You believe this?'

'You know this. We often spoke of it when you were alive. Our victory. We fought and won the second *Chimurenga*, and we established a vanguard party to course this country onto a Socialist footing. We destroyed our enemies. The British and American Imperialists tried to halt the slow revolution of our democracy, our freedom, our sovereignty, but we have defeated them.'

The words seem papery now, empty of meaning. Repeated too many times. Like stones falling from his mouth.

'The witness does not lie, Robert.'

The guards outside the door do not hear this man's cackling laughter. The President dares not cry out loud, though he wants to. 'Why do you come to mock me? Haven't I paid you back in full?'

The *chipoko* shows the same wounds that he was found with at the bottom of the ravine in Mozambique. A gruesome tear across his face, still bleeding. Won't it ever heal, that wound? It's been forty years, for God's sake. 'I am the rightful ruler of Zimbabwe,' he says, 'and you think you can brush me off like this?'

'I was found innocent of those charges. I was blameless. It was a car accident. You always drove recklessly. And that day in Mozambique...'

'You dare contradict me?'

'Tekere publicly came out and told them I did not do it...'

'Tekere is a drunken fool. An April Fool.'

'I have done all you said.'

'You want to rule forever? What vain myths you cling to, Robert! You think you can stop history, you who once rode on its frothy waves? You are like the grinning fool who pulls the table cloth down on him; the country has tumbled and crashed because you insisted on clinging to power with your yellow fingernails. But the end is soon. We are all waiting for you. All the dead.'

The President tries to smile. 'There have been many rumours of my death. But I am still here.'

'This may be your last night, Robert.'

And the man is gone.

He lies awake that night, but at midnight drops into a deep slumber in his armchair. As usual, the nightmares visit him. But this night it is different. Tonight he finds himself driving a black funeral hearse to Heroes Acre, and in the back is a coffin, draped with a Zimbabwe flag. It is a state funeral, and the road ahead is lined with dignitaries – Joshua Nkomo, Ndabaningi Sithole, Rex Nongo, Lookout Masuku, and Solomon Mujuru. And Josiah Tongogara, who winks at him. There is Samora Machel, and look, even Ian Smith is here. There is his wife Sally, talking to another woman – oh it's Susan Tsvangirai. And down the road, his old friends. Nicolai Ceausescu, and there, look – Muammar Gaddafi.

He drives slowly, but the car speeds up, past hundreds of soldiers. He should pay attention to where he is going, because the road becomes a steep mountain pass, sloping down into a vast blue hazy valley. He touches the brakes lightly, but there is no response, so he presses the pedal with a firm foot. Nothing happens. The car speeds up, faster and faster past the crowds – down the steep mountain pass. He stamps on the pedal. He tries to change gears, and the car screams but does not slow.

The speedometer is showing one hundred kilometres an hour, two hundred, three hundred. Ahead of him he sees the end of the road: a cliff edge, and below, the Honde Valley, pimple mounds of mountains, the plains of Mozambique below him. The crowds watch him whizz past, waving flags that bear his image, ululating, as he plunges over the edge and tumbles into the air, slowly, then faster and faster. The earth is coming up to meet him, that red earth, and he sees granite boulders piled up in impossible formations getting closer and closer as he speeds down, falling, falling, falling.

31 Murdering Creek Road

They moved into 31 Murdering Creek after his dad left. Just the two of them. The five-bedroomed house was sinking into the mire of its own past. But Mrs. Murtoa, the owner, had offered it up for such low rent after her messy divorce, they couldn't say no. The Queenslander stood on sinking poles. The wrap-around balcony had rotted; the high ceilings sagged and leaked, the rooms downstairs stank of ornate decay; the doors from the living room to the veranda didn't open because the house sagged at both ends.

He called his room the Train Room. It looked like a station waiting room; the roof had been painted mustard yellow; the walls were maroon with green trim. His mother took the main bedroom on the other side of the house.

Every morning at five, a million stridently cheerful lorikeets landed on the blocked gutters on the roof and bathed in the standing water, splashing it into the rising sun. Six kookaburras waited in a neat line on the balcony by the kitchen, growling for balls of raw mince. One would let him stroke its head and scratch the lice on its scalp. Two currawongs visited every day, took food from his fingers. Sulphur-crested cockatoos crash-landed on the deck to crack the seeds he scattered for them.

The 1.89 acre garden was, he discovered, an unusable swamp that sloped into a creek and drained into Lake Weyba, a salt lake only a few centimetres deep that rose and fell with the tide. At king tides the brothy estuary lapped at the bottom fence of the property. His mother forbade him to go anywhere near the stream that leaked like pus from the boil of the garden. And this primeval stench, for a thirteen-year-old boy, attracted him like a tragic flaw.

That first night, his mother locked everything tight, but around midnight, he heard the squeak of a door opening.

Then a little after one, something cracked right below his bedroom, downstairs. He pulled the sheets over his head, and waited. An hour later, he heard the thump of a body on the tin roof, more thumps, and then something – or someone – rolling off and crashing into the bushes.

In the morning, he inspected the locked doors. 'Mum, were you walking around last night?'

'It's just the house breathing,' she said. 'And did you hear that possum on the roof?'

'I heard a gunshot downstairs.'

'These old Queenslanders expand and contract, and the walls crack as it cools. Here.' She led him down into the basement: a long crack snaked down the wall.

'Who were the previous occupants? Were they... murdered?'

'Don't be silly. The previous occupants are still alive. You met her – Mrs Murtoa.'

'Who was, then?'

'Who was what?

'Never mind.'

He fingered the crack in the wall. Cracks are like arguments, he thought, splitting families apart.

In the first week, and then subsequently every week after that, Mr. Fix-It the builder from Yandina arrived in a Ute piled with tools and machines and drills and wet vacuum cleaners, and whistled his way to the front door, to fix the leaking roof, or water pump, or guttering, or whatever.

'She wants to sell this place as quickly as possible,' the man explained as he hammered and sawed and drilled. 'It's costing her a pretty penny, but she wants it all fixed up.'

'Mrs Murtoa assured us that we could stay as long as we needed,' said his mother.

'You're not interested in buying the place, are you?' The builder's eyes were sharp.

The boy's mother shook her head. 'We can't afford anything at the moment.'

'How much does she want for it?' the boy asked.

'Asking over seven.'

'Seven hundred?

'Seven hundred thousand, darling,' his mother said. She turned to the builder. 'We're waiting for the sale of our old house to go through, so we can't even think of buying yet. And even then, we wouldn't be able to afford anything over four.'

The boy clutched his mother's hand. 'You don't want to buy this place, do you?'

'Of course not.'

But he grew to like the decay, the sagging bedroom wings, the nightly possum thudding on the roof, the widening crack in the walls which he measured every day, calculating how long it would take to reach the other side of the room. He liked the stream that oozed sulphur. And in visceral proportion he grew to hate the builder, who would arrive unannounced at odd hours, surprising his mother who had to open the door clutching her night gown. 'I've come to seal the cracks' (in vain because they simply widened the minute he left and spat out his filler and paint with dismissive contempt); 'I've come to fix the leaking toilet' (but I like the dripping sound, whined the boy); 'How is the shower head now, Mrs Watson, giving you a good hot shower?'

'Does he have to be here at eight in the morning? On Saturday?'

'Someone has to maintain the place,' she said. 'And he has to deal with the termites.'

The termites had eaten the central beam of the house, and the upper bathroom had collapsed in a pile of moist wood shavings. The boy could hear them at night.

'Want to see a termite colony?' The builder called him into the basement bedroom and scraped away the paint on the roof beam. Clotted dirt fell out of what used to be wood, and white grubs scurried away. The man squeezed one between his fingers. 'These little buggers will destroy the whole place in no time. I'll have to spray and replace the beam.' And with one pinch he squished the termite.

'Don't kill them,' the boy said.

The next day, Mr. Fix-It sprayed and injected poison into the walls and dug a trench of death around the house.

'This will cost her,' he said. 'And she wants the cracks gone. We'll have to re-stump the whole house if she's going to sell it.'

The boy's mother managed to negotiate a stay of execution. 'Not while we're in it, you can't.'

'We'll have to wait until you move out then.' He winked at her.

And then the boy came back from school to find his room – his maroon and green and mustard train room – covered in canvas sheets and stinking of paint, and the builder touching up the ceiling with a dripping roller brush.

'She wants the room white,' he said. 'It's this room that puts buyers off. Sorry, I had to move your junk out for now.'

'I don't want it white,' the boy said to his mother. 'Tell him to put it back the way it was.'

'It's not our house, darling. We're just renting.'

The builder couldn't fix the door to the veranda. The cracks he had painted over showed through the layers of white.

'Yes, show him, house!' said the boy.

Every day the yellow eyed currawongs circled the house cawing for food; every night the wall cracked and the floorboards creaked. The ghost creeping around at night was the spirit of the house itself. And he could feel its shape around him, like a father's embrace.

Every day he inspected the cracks, managing to insinuate his pinkie inside its crumbling coolness. Twenty centimetres to go.

Six months came and went. The 'For Sale' sign outside attracted a few potential buyers, but the boy soon chased them away by hauling the heavy furniture off the stained carpets, by pointing out the termite-eaten beams in the basement, the rotten deck, and the rusty mower drowned in the mud at the end of the garden. Would-be buyers mired themselves in the swampy earth, fingered the widening cracks in the walls, and made hurried and polite retreats.

The boy and his mother were safe.

And then Auntie Doris and her two kids came to stay. It was such a big house, his mum said, and they needed help with the rent. 'You don't mind sharing the space with Gina and Rebecca do you? Gina's almost thirteen, so you should get on well.'

'As long as I keep the train room.'

The visitors stayed in the downstairs self-contained flat where the concrete exploded every night. 'Where's your father?' he asked Gina.

'Her father is in Fiji,' answered the six-year-old Rebecca. 'My father is from Africa.'

'She's never seen her father,' said Gina. 'Mine still visits now and then. But it's better when he doesn't. What about yours?'

'He's just in the UK for a while,' the boy said. 'Needs some time to work things out. But he'll be back soon.'

It only took a day or so. Then he took Gina to his secret places. He trusted her black eyes and her ironic smile; she hated the builder just because he did. He showed her the man-cave garage where the previous owner had left all his stuff, including a TV and video with some old porn videos, the attic where the carpet python surrounded himself with his shed snake skins, and the laundry chute that they managed to stuff Rebecca down so she landed on the pile of dirty clothes downstairs.

Together they prised open the crack with eager fingers. And later, he took her to Murdering Creek. Rebecca trailed after them.

'I'll show you my secret place, the actual place where people were murdered, why it's called Murdering Creek.'

Rebecca followed. 'Not you!' said Gina. 'This is a really scary place, not for kids.'

Rebecca squelched after them. The water stank. The boy stood on roots that were trying to breathe through the mud, and clay squished between his toes. He led them down the creek to a clearing that opened out into the lake.

'Cool.' Gina walked right in. 'It's so warm, it's like a bath.'

'This is where they were murdered.'

'Who? Who was murdered?' called a tiny voice behind them.

'You, if you don't stop following us.'

He pointed out the triangular imprints of rays that had rested on the clay bottom. 'Weyba means ray,' he said. 'They used to hunt emu here and fish. Peregian means emu.'

He showed her the scar trees, the stone fish traps, and the paper bark tree growing in the shallows, its roots clutching the bank to stop getting pulled out by the tide. 'This is where I come to think.'

They sat like leopards in the branches, dangled their feet in the water, and watched the anxious rhythm of the waves lapping at the roots.

'It's beautiful. So quiet.'

'It's creepy,' called Rebecca from the shore.

'Ignore her.'

They watched Rebecca meander off into the thickets where fallen paper barks made neat bridges across the creek. They listened to the far away roar of the ocean, the tide against them, swayed like trees in the hot breeze. 'Look!' A sting ray floated below in the shallows, its fins rippling. They watched clouds reflected in the water. They listened to the silence of the past.

And then:

'Aren't you ever going to kiss me?' said Gina.

He was not sure how to answer. 'OK.'

He had never thought of kissing her. They balanced on a fork in the tree, and the knots pushed into his back as she pressed herself against him. He was dizzy enough to fall off, and had to clutch the branches with his hands to steady himself. Paper bark flaked off in his hands like pages from an old book.

'That's enough,' she said.

'Disgusting,' came a voice from below.

'Rebecca! Go away, you little shit.'

'I'll tell ma.' Running now, she hurled the words back at them. 'I'll tell her you two were fucking.'

Gina's face was dark. 'She doesn't even know what the word means.' She leaped off the tree, splashed across the shallows and Rebecca howled and plunged into the bushes. The boy heard them splashing up the stream and Gina pounding after her all the way back to the house.

The builder sat perched on the roof. 'Damn bird shit everywhere up here,' he said. 'Have to replace this whole goddamn gutter.'

'They're my pets,' the boy said, but not loud enough for the builder to hear him. 'Leave them alone.'

He thumped inside to find Rebecca cradled in her mother's arms, sucking her thumb. 'What happened?'

Gina winked at him. 'Nothing.'

'Oh, use the downstairs shower,' said his mother. 'The builder is fixing ours.'

The boy never believed him. Never trusted him. There was always some repair job; he was always there, surprising them at odd moments, even catching Gina in the toilet one day (sorry! sorry! I had no idea you were in here! The tiles. Sorry, sorry!), or outside his mother's bedroom fixing the louvres, or banging at the bay window while the boy tried to do Maths, as if deliberately trying to stop him thinking.

And there he was, the builder, having tea with the boy's mother outside. He was having none of it. 'Any news from Dad?'

'No, no,' she said. 'He needs more time.'

'He's had ten months. And three days.'

'Please, darling, I need to discuss something very important here with the builder.'

The house loved him now, he knew, and would do anything to protect him. It had embraced Gina too. He could not imagine how he had hated it when he first arrived. It was trying to speak to him, and he had learned its language. He loved the Huntsman spiders in the corners of every room where you could not quite reach with a duster, the cockroaches in the cupboards, and the dark basement where Gina and he played and hid from Rebecca whose wails filled the echoing empty rooms. They would stuff her down the laundry chute and threaten to block both ends and leave her there.

He loved the creek now, saw how its colour was the same gleaming yellow of the currawong's eyes. Liked its raw name. Liked the stench of death. He dangled the name in front of his two friends like a talisman.

It drove Rebecca crazy. 'Who was murdered there? Tell me. Tell me. Tell me.'

Even Gina wanted to know. He had teased them for months, but he now knew he couldn't ever tell them what he knew, what he had read on the Internet about Murdering Creek.

'Nobody,' he said.

He knew it was coming. But he didn't know it would be so soon. 'They've given us an ultimatum,' said his mother. 'We have to leave or else buy the house.'

'Why can't we keep renting it?'

'Mrs Murtoa has to sell it. She wants us out to do major repairs. Stumping, fixing the deck, repainting the house. She thinks having us in it is giving a bad impression to buyers.'

Auntie Doris sighed. 'We could pool our resources. And didn't your house sell?'

'Four hundred.'

'We can offer five, then.'

'They'll never take five. After all the work the builder has put into it. He says he's put at least fifty thousand's worth of work in already. She wants seven at least.'

'Make them a cheeky offer.'

In the end, his mother and Auntie Doris offered five hundred thousand. 'It's so run down, and termites have eaten half the basement,' she said. 'And it's cracked and rotten.'

The builder shook his head. 'She won't even deign that with a response. But I'll pass on the message.'

He was right: Mrs Murtoa never responded. 'She's totally insulted,' his mother said. 'We shouldn't have made such a low offer. But what can we do?'

'We can't leave,' said the boy.

'I'm sorry, darling.'

'But,' he said, 'the crack hasn't even reached the corner of the room yet.'

The builder was ripping up the mouldy carpets even as they were hauling boxes out of the rooms. By the time they were driving off, all their belongings huddled in the *Van Go* truck, he had already pulled off the gutters, and piled up rotten pieces of deck. Lorikeets circled the house in distress, and the currawongs watched from a tree with swamp eyes.

The yellow wound in him opened. It would never heal. Never.

'It's just a house,' said his mother. 'Not a person. Just a house.'

Auntie Doris, Gina and Rebecca moved in with relatives in Brisbane.

He and his mother squeezed into a box-house in Tewantin next to other boxes where people played thumping bass and mowed all day and where you could hear fathers shouting at mothers in confined spaces.

'We must tell Dad our new address so he knows where to find us – when he returns.'

'Yes, of course.'

In the local newspaper he saw the house listed – For Sale, 700,000 – and stared at the fish-eyed photos of a house that looked new, bright, with hard wood floors in the living room, new steel gutters; white, white rooms with no chandeliers or spiders in the ceilings.

A month later, he saw the same photos of the house with a red SOLD sticker pasted over them with too many excited exclamation marks.

He was surprised at his mother's tears when he showed her: SOLD $500, 000.

'Look Ma,' he said.

'It's all right. It's all right.'

'Don't cry, Ma.'

Six months later they drove past the house for a garage sale at the end of Murdering Creek Road. He didn't want to look, but as they slowed down near the house, he saw the Ute in the driveway. A white dog barking at the gate. The builder sitting out on his new deck, feet up, whistling.

The boy cried and cried and cried.

The Flat

In the city of Durban, KwaZulu-Natal, (in the imaginary country of Azania, Afrika,) a man rented an apartment, (or 'flet' as we call it here), near the beach, in a derelict but expensive area behind Point Road. The area had been a whites-only area, and was still a largely whites-only area due to the exorbitant rents set by unscrupulous and invisible landlords. I'm only talking of the insides of the apartments, of course: the streets were the habitat of prostitutes and street children. The man (let me call him a Modern Afrikanist for now) rented the flat and lived alone, which was unusual, but for reasons not part of this story, had the money to be able to afford this lifestyle.

The flat afforded a sea-view, or so the landlord had told him. The apartment block was crowded in with other dilapidated buildings, but if he craned his neck out of the kitchen window on a clear day, he could see a blue patch of sea between the Nedbank towers and The Wheel. Taxi-drivers, prostitutes and street brawlers below made the street a noisy place at night, but once he had bolted and double-locked his front door and slammed the street-facing windows, the Modern Afrikanist would be left in silence to pursue his artistic endeavours.

Unfortunately, the main feature of this flat was not its privacy, but the scuttling of feelers, and rasping of carapaces against the linoleum. In Durban, cockroaches grew to four to five inches long. He would find them everywhere: coming out of taps, boiled in the kettle when he made tea, gorging themselves in the sugar bowl, sleeping disguised as Honey Smacks in his tightly sealed cereal packets... he didn't like squashing them – such a gooey mess. He spread toxic white powder for them in the kitchen cupboards; he plugged up the taps; he sealed his food. But

51

yet they kept coming. He resorted to spraying the crevices, cracks and border runners to his flat every morning before he went out to work, and then would return at night to find piles of cockroach corpses in the bath, on the kitchen table, in the bed, and lining the skirting board to every room.

His initial repugnance soon grew into a hesitant fascination for these armies of determined creatures, who by their suicidal insistence, claimed residence here. Over supper (Bunny Chow bought from The Star of India Take-Away downstairs), he found himself staring at a particularly large dead cockroach on its back on the dining table. With its serrated legs, its oval shape, the light reflecting purple and orange off its back, it spoke to him. I am black, but comely, it said. Behold, I also am formed out of the clay.

He was instantly ashamed. The Modern Afrikanist was an artist: he prided himself on an aesthetic relation to the world: so why should he exclude cockroaches from his artistic apprehension of the universe? They had value. They had form. They had beauty.

The gleam in his eye was inspiration, artistic inspiration. Instead of brushing away the dead cockroach in disgust, he set up easel and paints on the table, and began painting its portrait, with garish Fauvist colours, and generous gobs of paint, smeared on with the gusto and urgency of Van Gogh.

Pleased with his evening's work, he hung the picture on the living room wall, and stood back to admire it. The next day the cockroach was still there. After breakfast, he shaped in clay a giant Rodin representation of the dead creature, and fired it in the oven.

And as he was loath to throw away this cockroach, he instead varnished it with a fine lacquer brush, and set it on the mantelpiece under his painting. And from hereon, he no longer swept away dead cockroaches, but collected and sorted them according to size, texture, colour, and position. He pasted the tiny ones onto a canvas and painted them – literally painted their backs in bright blue, orange and green – into a landscape, and hung it on the wall in his kitchen. Monet would be impressed: up close, the painting was a knobbly packed death trench of cockroaches; from a distance, one saw the North KwaZulu coast line, with sweeping, wavy cane fields, a few workers dotted in the stalks and smoke rising in the distance where old cane fields were being burned off.

He glued the large cockroaches along the rim of his bookcase to make a pleasing pattern of ridges and bumps, taking care with the feelers so they would form a pattern of aerial lightness.

As more and more cockroaches died, he collected them all, painstakingly, and created more works of art. In a short few weeks, he covered all his furniture with varnished cockroach designs; seven magnificent paintings hung on his walls, and three large statues sat on his tables in raw clay, an essential gesture of cockroach emerging out of the formlessness of his previous prejudices. Soon there were no more walls to use: he covered his lampshade with cockroach designs; he made a sofa cover from the smooth corpses of cockroaches; he covered his desk with the oval pattern; he pasted them all over the bookcase. He loved cockroaches now – their form, their slender shape, their nestling together. A million new projects spun from his mind onto paper in the middle of the night – a cockroach-paste sculpture, a cockroach doorway, a cockroach carpet.

Ironically, after a month, he ran out of cockroaches. Either there were no more in the dark spaces behind the walls of his flat, or they had got wind of his intentions, and had migrated to better homelands, where they had more to eat, and where macabre, varnished corpses of their brothers and sisters did not stare at them from walls and bookshelves and headboards.

But the Modern Afrikanist still bubbled with inspiration; and so he went out in search of raw material. He scoured the rubbish containers at the end of the street and collected roaches in plastic bags lined with white powder. He frequented the back end of The Star of India restaurant, the stench of a make-shift toilet behind the shish-kebab stall on the corner, and the stair wells of his apartment building. He fell into conversation with taxi-drivers late at night while prowling at the back of the Wheel entertainment complex. 'Excuse me,' he said to a sex worker, picking up a scuttling dark creature from under her high-heel and popping it into his bag; or 'Do you mind...?' to a schwarma-eating customer as he spied a scuttling scavenger in the paper wrapper. If only he could breed the cockroaches himself! But there was no need: he arrived home every evening with sacks full, sorted them out by shape and breed (brown, black, Asian, Smoky-Brown), glued broken feelers on the big ones, repaired broken wings, legs, and carapaces, then set to work.

The paintings looked beautiful: the Indian Ocean he couldn't quite see from the kitchen window; clear skies, zero humidity, the brown smog that skulked over Durban vanquished; the street below, devoid of prostitutes and taxis and street gangs, replaced by a post-Apartheid rainbow community; a self-portrait of a clear-faced, hopeful Modern Afrikanist, looking out onto the horizon of the African Renaissance. Each painting breathed hope into the world, of hopeful futures, of the Afrika he loved and embraced.

One day, however, the modern Afrikanist found a dead cockroach in the bottom of his Coke can, and spat out feelers, legs and body juices. He had been drinking dead cockroach; no wonder it had tasted bitter.

He was no great discerner of colas. He drank Coke and Pepsi with equal lack of discrimination. He lived, oblivious to the subtleties of the images associated with each, produced by the multinational corporations in attempts to get people to think they were buying good times, the real thing, popularity, the Modern African way, when all they were doing was buying carbonated water with caffeine, inverted corn syrup (sugar in KwaZulu Natal because of its plentiful supply), phosphorus, and bad teeth. When he could, he tried to get Royal Crown Cola, the remembered favourite from his childhood bottle store in Ulundi. He had even tried Dr Pepper, but found it too artificial, too plasticky, too American.

From here on, he liked to think of Coke/Pepsi as liquidised cockroach – black and fizzy, just as he imagined a crushed cockroach would taste. It resulted in the acidic burning in this stomach that concentrated cockroach would produce. He drank Coke or Pepsi when he painted, sculpted, drew, and used it for inspiration, its destructive, invasive foreignness militating against his stomach juices. And this is how he celebrated the process of art.

But just when he was getting into the swing of things, the Modern Afrikanist's flat was again invaded. The cockroaches had been absent for so long, that his nightly excursions had become routine. At first he delighted to see his prodigal creatures return and celebrated by watching them scuttle over his food, out of his taps. But as they grew more and more voluminous, he decided to dust them down with white powder.

It did not work. He found too many of them, or maybe they had grown immune, adapting to their hostile environment, and they looked a new breed, a more determined wave of invaders who had strategised and schemed, and planned their defiance campaign. Even though he carted out hundreds of dead cockroaches every day, even more live ones returned with a vengeance. They poured into the flat from all those crevices, from all those secret places up in the rafters, behind the walls, in the dark cistern cupboard, through tunnels that led from the streets below, up the air conditioning vents, along water pipes, through garbage chutes. He had plenty of material for his art now, and what's more, a crisis, a disruption to his art, which would itself make great art, but he needed time, reflection and distance in order to produce it. And of this he had none.

Cockroaches carry diseases, he reminded himself. They cause food poisoning (both Salmonella and Escherichia), Leprosy, bubonic plague, typhoid, parasitic worms (Helminths). It is for good reason that they are loathed. What had he been thinking all this time?

When he woke one day with cockroach feelers on his face, his flirtation with experimental cockroach art was over. He returned that evening with three cans of Roachkill III. Cockroaches scuttled all over the kitchen: on the bread, in the packets of sandwiches, in the pots, indignantly upset when he stamped his feet at them; they only retreated a short distance then returned, these impunitious creatures.

He sprayed clumps of cockroaches, descending on them in surprise, covering them with glistening insecticide, and then watched grimly as they writhed, kicked and stammered their farewell to this world in their raspy cockroach voices.

Where had his compassion gone? His response was reflexive. Them or me. But once he had emptied all three containers onto large clumps, into illegal gatherings of cockroaches, they still came. They still were fearless. They knew they could outlive him. Even when he hurled the empty cans at them, they didn't scatter, a few of them clambering onto the yellow design of dead cockroaches on the cans themselves.

The Modern Afrikanist hadn't gotten rid of them but he had certainly taught them a lesson. They would flee when they heard his footsteps. He would spy them quivering in cracks. All those cracks! There must be millions of cockroaches living behind these walls. What a fool he was to think this was place of sanctuary, when under his floorboards he could hear them scrabbling and writhing and clawing at each other in the dark. There were just too many holes. Just when he thought he had a cockroach cornered, it would mysteriously vanish into a crack in the skirting board. Then it would appear somewhere else. Had this block of flats been built on a dark crypt of loathsome prehistoric creatures, sealed for centuries and now open to the modern world?

That day he bought more Roachkill and a bag of polyfilla, determined to seal them out of his living space. But still they came. He pasted white filler all along the skirting board over every crack, up on the ceilings, along crevices, but still they came. He would wake up at night to hear them having a party in his kitchen. He sealed the breeze blocks in the walls; he sealed windows tightly at night; he wedged paper under the door, and still somehow they got in.

He would get up at night, switch on the light in the kitchen and spray blindly all over. They learned that at no time they were safe, unless they heard the front door bang as he left the flat. Sometimes he would surprise them by leaving, but then return a few minutes later to find them already at his food. He swept piles of the dare devils into corners as a lesson to the others. He had lost the ability to see them as creatures of wonder. He had ceased to paint.

As the days went on, his victory was assured. His throat grew dry, but he had to keep up the spraying – the cockroaches were relentless and to slow down now would be to show weakness. His eyes brimmed red, and he had developed a wheeze and a hollow cough. He slept very lightly, afraid that a cockroach might crawl over him. And when he did sleep deeply, he dreamed that they crawled all over his body, their jagged feet tickling him, burrowing into his crotch, snuggling under his arms to nestle.

Then he fell sick: he had obviously picked up a bug of sorts from these vile creatures who had been crawling all over his food. Even his breadbin was not safe. He sprayed it inside and out. Cockroach symptoms spread throughout his body: fever, sore throat, squelching stomach, which not even the Coke could soothe. Every time he ate something, he had to rush to the toilet, spray the insects aside, and squeeze out cockroach coloured stools of digested cockroach. He stared in disgust at the liquidised cockroach his body had produced in the bowl, and flushed it, scrubbed it, sprayed it. Had they been crawling in his mouth while he slept? That would explain the twitchy feeling in his stomach, as if dozens of jagged feet were scrambling through his tubes of digesting food. The essence of cockroach grew inside him. Worse than dreaming of being a cockroach, they had inhabited him, spitting on their food to digest it (or was that flies) then he ate it, this yellow cockroach diarrhoea on everything he touched – in his bath, on the toilet seat, on his plates, in his glasses, in the very air he breathed.

For days he languished in bed in a fever, tossing, throwing up, voiding his bowels… feeling imaginary legs running over him. He would burn with rage to hear them scuttling in the kitchen, taking advantage of his weak condition. He would crawl, can in hand, into the kitchen or bathroom or wherever, spray them then fall into a hot sleep, only to dream of them coming pouring out of holes in the wall, shitting on his food, salivating on his food, sawing their feelers together in glee.

But he had a new plan: starve the buggers out. If he had no food in the house, if he fasted for 48 hours, he would cure himself of diarrhoea and they'd have to go somewhere else. He cleared the kitchen of all foodstuff, sprayed empty bins and cupboards, and kept only bottles of Coke in the fridge, which he sipped weakly every now and then, homoeopathically, this effervescent spirit of cockroach. He drank and drank, hoping to purge himself of this evil. Bubbles prickled down his throat, gas bloated his stomach, he belched foul smelling cockroach breath, and farted loud cockroach smells.

The next day he was weaker. He decided to stay in bed, nurture his delusions, and the hunger artist he was, decided to create works of art from the visions that came from his condition. But all he could do was watch limply as one cockroach after another crept out into his room, emboldened by his condition. They hadn't found any food, the bastards, yet they came sniffing, feeling their way, whatever it was they did. Another poked its way out of a crevice he thought he'd filled up. And another. Yet another. He watched, paralysed with hate, but with underlying triumph – he had the can of spray in his hand. Gather his strength. As he reached for the can, a few cockroaches hesitated then continued their business tormenting him... He sat up slowly, found the nozzle, and unable to keep from smiling, aimed, pressed. Nothing happened. Spray seeped onto his hand, then air. He shook the can, tried again. The spray of air died away like a last breath. The cockroach scuttled at his first act but didn't hide. It sensed his powerlessness. He flung the useless can against the wall. A cockroach nearby inspected it. He could count five-six-seven, now eight large cockroaches – big black shiny ones – ten, twelve, long as a finger, fat as a sparrow.

Leave me alone, he shouted, you've punished me enough. Go away. Cockroaches hear, as we know, only through vibrations felt through their legs. They didn't respond. Then he felt a quiver on the sheets, and there was a cockroach by his feet. He kicked out and the cockroach was hurled into the air, and writhed on the floor on its back. But then it flapped a pair of horrible insect wings and flew. It flew! He never knew cockroaches could fly. It vibrated science fiction story wings, flew past him and landed on the wall behind his bed. He banged clumsily on the wall behind to unsettle it, tried to flick the cockroach away with his comb. But it spread its paper-thin wings again and flew into the living room.

He had one last bottle in the kitchen. He dragged himself to the counter, banged away the roaches clustering on the counter, and pulled it weakly down. He was not going to waste it squirting onto individual cockroaches, or into the air. He had to protect himself. Cockroaches were now flying around the room, given free reign. He sprayed the repellent all over him: legs, arms, face, chest. That would keep them away. He sprayed clean and hard so the spray was greenish liquid drenching his skin. It was good. It would cleanse him. He began with his feet up his legs, groin – it stung horribly here, but it had to be done – stomach, back, arms, neck, and face. He screwed up his eyes but a lot still got into his nose and ears. Eyes burned. He sprayed his lips heavily: if any cockroaches dared to get near here… His throat burned like fire, his stomach turned in revolt – all those nasty creatures inside after his food. His skin cried out, but now he was safe. His tongue had the bitter taste of diethltoyande. His nose ran, his eyes watered and smarted, but in glee he watched triumphantly as the cockroaches drew closer to the bed. They were in for a surprise. Sudden death would overtake them. Then he lay still waiting for sleep, breathing uneasily. He imagined being found dead the next morning by the caretaker of the flat, who wanted his three months' unpaid rent: cause of death – cockroach poisoning, but he preferred the thought that the cockroaches would carry him away and devour him bit by bit until they too choked and died, all of them, all the millions behind the walls, all with human diarrhoea.

Cicadas

9:30 pm, June 14 1986

Saturday evening, both Magoo's and the adjacent Why Not bar on Marine Parade are packed like cattle trucks on the way to slaughter houses. The smoke, the crowds, the late nights – this is what we do on Saturday nights – Sean, Gina, Janet, Alan, Caryn – sensitive white intellectuals, anti-Apartheid activists, all of us.

See, that's me, John, dancing in a circle with Caryn, Gina and Sean. Sean in his tight blue jeans and Durban floral shirt thrashes about the dance floor, eyes shining, beer bottle in his hand. His shaved head bobs above the crowds. Gina has assigned herself his partner tonight, though she is officially a Lesbian. Caryn is with me. We are all ideological bedfellows. We inhabit the English Department graduate lounge, we hold fervent discussions, drink coffee, suck on cigarettes, and study Lukacs, Jameson, Bakhtin, Gramsci. We demonstrate against the Apartheid regime, organise rallies, sign petitions, denounce white liberals. We're activists. And that makes us very cool. A minority white anti-Apartheid group. Very Cool.

But Sean, Alan, Tom, Steven, me – we're white males. And in 1986 that puts us in a predicament. All white males, when they leave school or university, are called up for two years to serve their country, to patrol townships, to spit teargas at demonstrating crowds, shoot rubber bullets into the backs of fleeing protesters, fight terrorists at the border; in short, defend an illegal Apartheid State.

There are few options. And my friends have tried them all.

You can flee the country, if they let you out. Go into exile. Live out the war in Europe, waiting to return.

You can refuse to fight, and apply for conscientious

objector status. But this is a legal battle you can never win. You either have to go to jail, or if you're lucky, serve three years community service.

You can 'go underground,' just disappear, sever contact with family and friends, hope they won't find you.

Or you can simply grit your teeth and bite the bullet, and go into the army. Two years, and then it's over.

There are other options. You can shoot yourself in the foot, disable yourself so you're functionally ineligible for active service; you can feign insanity. You can commit suicide. You can have a sex change.

Radical options. We're radical, but not that radical.

Sean, for example, has spent the last four years at university declaring that he will never serve in the Apartheid military. So when he receives his call up papers, he announces at the student rally that he is going to flee into exile rather than face complicity and be called up to fight for a repressive regime. 'Never will I take up a gun to fight for Apartheid!' His voice echoes across campus. To great applause, he tears up his call up papers, and waves a one way ticket to London. But like many white South African males who have done this, he gets a rude shock in exile. He spends a grey winter huddled against a radiator, falls to suicidal depths he never knew he had. Why? The only significance in his life is the struggle, his home here, his friends, the cultural context. Remove him and he dies. Perhaps he begins to realise that his life here is built on pampered privilege.

So Sean is back. Never will I take up a gun to fight for Apartheid! But now he is going to do just that; he's been back in the country scarcely a week, and has to report for duty in two days at the military command base here in Durban.

He is talking loudly to us about exile, about the bleak

63

horrors of his last few months. He is glad to be back, even for a short few days.

Alan over there at the bar, decked out in black Goth apparel – silver earrings, cross, side burns, stove pipe Levi's – was called up weeks ago, and instead of answering the call of duty, he's simply going underground. Over there, Tom, with the large glasses that make him always look surprised, has decided to become a conscientious objector and fight it out in the courts. And Steven, dancing there in the corner, is feigning homosexuality, a slipped disk and schizophrenia.

And me you ask? What am I going to do? I have no fucking idea. So far I have deferred call ups, extending my studies as long as I can. The loophole: you can defer military service if you're studying at university. So here I am: B.A., B.A. Honours, Masters... Can I stretch this into a PhD? But it won't wash. They're refusing to let me go on. As soon as I hand in my dissertation, I'm theirs. But how long can you stretch an M.A. in postcolonial literature with special reference to the novels of JM Coetzee?

There are not many options for young black men either in 1986. Either you go along with the regime as a second class citizen who cannot vote, cannot control your destiny, cannot live, study or work where you want, or you can go into exile in some cold, sunless place. Or you can fight the regime – stand up against it, join the armed struggle, plant bombs, and hopefully avoid jail, torture, death.

At the age of 26, Robert McBride, better known in the white media of 1986 as the 'Durban Bomber' has made his choice. And his resume is already very impressive:

1. Rocket Attack on the Mobil Oil Refinery in Durban, 14 May 1984;
2. Attack on transformer at Musgrave Road, Durban,

21 June 1984;
3. Explosion of sub-station at Queen Mary's Avenue, Durban, 7 August 1984;
4. Explosion at sub-station at Gale Street, Durban on 14 September 1984;
5. Explosion of sub-station at Woodlands, Durban, 21 June 1985;
6. Umlazi Police Station – 10 February 1986;
7. Explosion of sub-station at Springfield, Durban, 12 February 1986;
8. Explosion of sub-station at Assagay, Hammersdale on 12 March 1986.

But his activist career is soon to be over.

9:50 pm, June 14 1986

There is no room in Magoos for all of us. We spill outside. To dance, you have to pack yourself in with others, breasts, hips, legs, hair flying in your face – humanity, cosy, tight, sweaty, of one mind. I am dancing with Caryn, if you can call this dancing. I have invited her to my flat afterwards. We have gone far enough down the path that neither of us can turn back even if we want to. We both know we will leave here at about midnight, maybe stop for a *schwarma* at the Taste of India café, walk back to my apartment in Point road. She will stay the night. The flat overruns with cockroaches and bad smells. Cockroaches pour out of taps, inhabit bread sealed in plastic bags, and even crawl in between the bed sheets. But she won't mind. She'll like the cockroach touch. It is part of her Bohemian rebellion against her bourgeois parents. She wears a UDF t-shirt over her braless breasts with a phalange of workers with a flag marching from the distant oppressive past into the glorious future. She has already told me she has herpes, which

65

means she has already entertained the possibility of sleeping with me.

We have had our disagreements, mostly political. The personal is political. It's not that we're not both radical, but she has a fixed doctrine, some Truth that I always slam up against whenever I question her. Some things cannot be questioned, like why we must sing *La Marseilleise* at rallies. Or why the makeshift study group must study Georg Lukacs. 'Why the hell should we? I ask. When I contradict her, she says, 'it's because you have a penis, isn't it? You think because you have a penis, you can have power over me.'

There will be no penetration, that's for sure: all penetration is rape. But I can expect sex of some sort. Sex is proof that we are liberated. That we are damaged beings seeking wholeness. And Caryn is as damaged as I am. That we do understand about each other. Her gestures are defensive, as if she has been hurt by many men, that she is not understood by her family, used to not being listened to. For my part, I am hesitant, self-obliterating, over sensitive. Her voice is a whine; mine is a stutter.

It's the Struggle, that's what this cosiness is: we are all in the Struggle. 'Are you in the struggle?' is the question you have to answer if you are to be part of this group. Having sex with someone in the struggle is a necessary requirement, a password.

10:00 pm, June 14 1986
The bomb will go off in fifteen minutes. The Durban bomber with two accomplices, Matthew Lecordier and Greta Apelgren, have parked the car outside the Why Not bar next door, primed the bomb, and have walked away out of earshot, so the report goes. They cannot malinger here too long, so they hang out near the police station.

In 1986, the policy of avoiding civilian casualties has apparently been somewhat relaxed in the armed struggle. Members of the South African Police frequent the 'Why Not Bar', and if we cannot get them in their Command centre, we can get them here. Let them know that they cannot hide behind civilians any longer.

Bombs have gone off in Durban before. Their effect is apocalyptic, the triumph of an advancing army. MK is here! each explosion announces. You can run but you cannot hide. Whiteys panic, scurry to their foxholes, or if they are lucky, Pack for Perth. Or even better, retaliate, escalate the war and enrage the masses until they wake from their slumber. The plume of smoke is worth a thousand words. You are not safe anywhere, it says, even in your laager.

10:05 pm, June 14 1986
Everyone from the university I know congregates here. *Hi, Hi, howzit,* I say in my clipped white South African accent. We all speak like this. I am a Masters student at University of Natal (Varsity we call it, or Durbs); I spend all my time not in the library or the Shepstone lecture halls, but in meetings in the Ref, chanting slogans, caught in the euphoria of a liberation movement where we all bond together and link arms – black, Indian, coloured, white. We whiteys march, carry banners, all indignant opponents of the evil Apartheid regime, and then we go home to our comfortable white areas protected from the black *gevaar* at night by the very policemen we throw stones at by day.

10:07 pm, June 14 1986
In 1986, you can still smoke in discos, so my eyes smart. I have to take constant breaks outside, walk across Marine Parade onto the beach for fresh air, and breathe in the briny

night. Women line the low wall outside, talking to each other about how things are going or not going with whoever and whomever. Some linger on the humid and misty streets, listen to the surf crash on the beach, and some stand three metres from the car which contains the ticking bomb.

And what a bomb! 100 pounds of explosives, machine-gun bullets in bags, and metal scraps for shrapnel – they really mean to hurt people.

I'm now dancing with Caryn alone in the corner of the room nearest the big glass windows. The song we are dancing to is Katrina and the Waves, Walking on Sunshine. The disco seems to float in the air, the people one writhing organism. Some mouth the words; others smile beatifically at each other, glazed with alcohol. I am trying to listen to Caryn's shrill conversation and have to stoop forward as she shouts in my ear. She's reading a Tom Robbins novel, she says. She loves it. She says it's like a giant orgasm from beginning to end.

'A what?'

'Orgasm.'

The dancing couple next to us smile in political collusion.

This is when I know I will sleep with her tonight, though how I will measure up to *Still Life with Woodpecker* I don't know. She wants me to read it. 'The premise of the novel is how to make love stay,' she says.

'Let's go outside for fresh air.' Her t-shirt is see-through with sweat, her nipples brown circles. 'Maybe just one more song; this one's my favourite…'

If we go outside, we will be two more fatal casualties of the bomb. It will change history. But we don't. It is not premonition; I am not psychic. It is because the song has changed to one I want to dance to: Kool and the Gang's 'Celebration.'

'Just because you have a penis doesn't give you the right to...'

10:15 pm, June 14 1986

Caryn does not finish. The glass shatters around us. I think my eardrums have burst. The room melts. The buoyant dancing mass sags. Glass spikes though the air. People fall like spiders in fire. Caryn's face and neck bloodies in front of my eyes. Time slows. Shards of glass fall in slow-motion, the roof caves, bricks tumble. Dust rises. It seems there is time for everything. I float to the floor, covering my head. Someone is kicking my ribs, someone else holding my legs in a rugby tackle. I huddle in foetal position, like those pictures of unborn babies on Anti-Abortion posters, waiting for time to start again.

It does. First I hear the screams, and then the terrible cracking of plaster and brick and glass. And then everyone stampedes for the exits. I look at Caryn's face, reach for her hand, pull her up. She stares at me, as if I-or my penis-is the cause of all this.

We squeeze through the sea of people outside. I cannot see Steve or Sean or Gina. The night air feels briny. I don't know what caused the explosion. The sirens latch onto the breeze and grow louder and more urgent.

I stagger to the curb, holding Caryn, her waist thick, her skin sweaty. She holds her face, and her hand is sticky. 'My God,' she keeps saying to me. I can smell the blood on her. In the streetlight, I check her eyes, ears, mouth, neck. 'You OK?'

'Of course I'm not fucking OK,' she says.

As far as I can make out, slivers of glass have wedged into her skin. It feels as if my face has been torn off, but she tells me there are only the same pieces of glass pimpled over my skin too. We walk on broken glass. A woman

69

writhes on the ground. I hear her screaming in the distance, though she is right beside me. One man buckled over the parapet is saying fuck, fuck, fuck over and over. The sirens are loud, now, too loud, and then they stop. The high beams of a police car flood the pavement, and a red light flashes onto the palm trees. In the trees, I hear the screech of cicadas.

Once I know I can see, smell, touch, and that Caryn is intact too, gratitude surges through me. Euphoria kicks in. I am important enough for life to happen to me, for someone to want to kill me. But then the shaking starts. 'It was a BOMB!' someone screams behind me. The neat carpet of life has been ripped up, the pavement pulled aside to reveal the emptiness underneath. What am I doing here, in Magoo's, in Durban, in Apartheid South Africa, when people wish me dead just for being alive?

'I'll take you to the hospital.' I say, but I cannot hear my words, the ringing in my ears is so loud.

'No way. I'm all right. I can stay at your place. Can I stay at your place?'

Ring. Ring. Wow. Flutter. I have to lip read.

'Are you sure you're OK?'

She dabs her wounds with a licked finger and then leans against me as we stagger down the street, two drunken love birds dripping with blood. Our feet tingle and do not quite touch the ground. My apartment is only four blocks away, on Point road, but it is a hell of a long way tonight. I push the front door open and cockroaches scuttle out of our path. I brush cockroaches off the basin, out of the tub and run her a bath. Naked, with a glass of wine in her hand, she slides into the steaming water. I kneel at the claw feet tub, and dab her wounds with a kitchen towel. Her breasts bob in the water. But I am focusing on glass fragments in her face and arms and legs. Nothing erotic here. No Tom Robbins moment. We are comrades, and her nakedness signifies nothing. Instead of lust, I am burning with self-pity. Why do they want to kill me? The arbitrary nature of the event stuns me. I believe in justice yes, an eye for an eye, yes, a just fight against Apartheid and its evil perpetrators of racial hate and crime, yes. But I am innocent, I want to tell the unknown bomber, the faceless ANC MK wing, the Enemy of the State. I am on your side, for Christ's sake. Where is the neat order of the Struggle where there are good guys and bad guys, and order and method, an upward march to freedom and liberation?

Caryn is brimming with self-righteousness. 'John, we all know who did this, don't we?'

'Sorry – I can't hear anything but wow and flutter.'

She exaggerates the words: 'We– all– know– who– did– this.'

'The Durban Bomber.'

'Don't be stupid. There's no such person…'

I dab the warm towel on her thighs, over her breasts, though there are no glass shards to dab.

'John, that's someone the media made up. It's the South African Police dirty tricks department. Typical of them. They knew the bar was full of radical lefties. Why else would they target that place?'

She has to repeat it again. Her words are underwater.

'I don't know. I can't live into the mind of someone who plants bombs to kill people.' She winces, as I pick out a glass splinter from her neck. Her legs are hot, unshaven, her arms red.

'To stir up hatred against the Struggle,' she bellows. 'To give them license to go after "terrorists". They've done it before. But this time they could kill two birds with one stone. Getting us lefties… and galvanise support.'

I know better than to argue. Contradiction is not simply

a disagreement; it is a denial of her being, her voice: a male attempt to rape, colonise, occupy territory, so I am careful what I say. But when I say it, I can hardly hear my own words. 'You must be right.'

'Are you OK?' She peers at my face.

'I just can't hear very well. Only ringing. Hiss. Do you hear the ringing?

'Yes. It'll pass.'

The next morning, the newspapers sizzle with outrage, and if you read carefully, intone gleefully at this confirmation and justification of their fears. 'Mad Durban Bomber Strikes Again'; 'Carnage in disco'; 'Bomb rocks Durban.' The word of choice is the verb 'rocks' – associated more with cuddles and cradles, or bands at large concerts than bombs. Even *The Weekly Mail* this time is allowed to print the news: Three Dead, 67 Injured in Bomb Blast. I am not sure if they counted us among the wounded.

Caryn heals fast. Apparently I sheltered her from the blast. Shards everywhere. In my flesh. Deep. The doctor has to remove some with anaesthetic and surgical incisions. Others I pluck out myself. But every time I sit down or lean against a wall or chair, I feel a stab of pain. I am, for a few months, a glass pincushion.

But my ears are the problem. I hear cicadas, loud throbbing, pulsing, loudest at night, when the world is quiet, when real cicadas sing in the trees outside my Point Road flat. It's hard to tell which are mine and which aren't.

I can stretch my dissertation on post-colonialism and the novels of JM Coetzee no longer. Within weeks, I receive a letter requesting me to present myself for a medical examination at Natal Command. And then I am rejected by the South African Defence Forces on the grounds of the cicadas in my ear. Unfit for Active duty, reads the memo. I'm deaf.

'Are you happy?' asks the Doctor who examines me, signs the report that exempts me from complicity with the regime.

'Will the cicadas stop?'

He shakes his head. 'The blast causes violent changes in air pressure that ruptured your eardrum and broke delicate bones inside your inner ear. The damage, I'm afraid, is permanent. The scars from the glass shards will heal, but you will hear cicadas for the rest of your life.'

The Durban Bomber is arrested and sentenced to death three times over for the bloody events of 1985 and 1986 which turned Durban into 'bomb city.' But after the Apartheid regime crumbles, before the death sentence can be carried out, Nelson Mandela pardons him. In 2004, Robert McBride, Matthew Lecordier and Greta Apelgren sit at the table of the Truth and Reconciliation Commission hearings. The judges want to find out if this attack was politically motivated, in which case it is pardonable; or if it is a crime, in which case it is not.

The case rests on the question whether military personnel frequented the bar, thus justifying an attack on 'the enemy'. If McBride can prove he targeted agents of Apartheid, then he has performed an honourable act of war. If not, he has grossly violated human rights.

'Why a bar full of civilians?'

McBride pleads a misjudgement in reconnaissance. A mistake. However, the TLC does manage to resurrect an old timer who had been in the police twenty years prior to his attendance at Magoo's that night.

McBride also pleads a change in ANC policy regarding

'soft targets.' From 1984, civilians became a legitimate target. The war against Apartheid now justified killing innocent supporters of the struggle apparently, who were by their very nature complicit.

McBride is acquitted, forgiven, absolved. The acts are clearly politically motivated. McBride becomes chief of the Metropolitan Police for Ekurhuleni Metropolitan Municipality. And in 2006, he receives the Merit Medal in Silver and the Conspicuous Leadership Star from the South African National Defence Force for his service and combat leadership in Umkhonto We Sizwe.

After twenty five years I'm still picking shards out of my flesh. At first I drew literal glass splinters from my face, my arms, my back, my legs. Some slid out easily; others left small septic pieces behind. And later, they were metaphorical. Beautiful crystals, spiky jewels.

Contrary to the adage, time doesn't heal old wounds: it leaves fibrous tissue that won't soften or ever let you forget. All these pock marks on my face tell a story, The Story, I tell over and over again, repeating the words until they too harden and scar. And the scars are medals, proof of history, a time when there were bombs and Struggles, and enemies and explosions.

The Magician's Son

'This seat taken?'

Without waiting for an answer, she flops onto the red bench seat next to him. He tries to ignore her. He presses his face to the bus window and watches the scraggly Msasa forests of the sub-tropical African Lowveld roll past him. She flicks a white wrist and pages through her *Fair Lady* magazine, licking her finger every time she turns the page, jabs her elbows and the magazine into his ribs. He scrunches his body as far from her as possible to give her room, but she sighs, twists, adjusts her bra. Blows out, lies back, stretches forward.

He yields to the inevitable. 'You're Katie Karbo. I've seen you on TV.'

'You know who I am? You watch Top of the Pops?'

Everyone knows who she is. Every Saturday night, she dances on TV to the number one Hit of the Week in a badly decorated studio on Pockets Hill in a badly choreographed routine with seven other scantily dressed dancers called the Silhouettes. Every Saturday night, she flicks her straw blonde long hair at the camera, shudders her bikinied breasts at the world, and flutters her Marilyn Monroe eyes at the male population. Of course he knows who she is.

'What are you doing on this trip?'

'I'm the magician's son.'

His father – who is chatting breezily to the blonde woman in the front row of the bus – is a magician, and he is the reluctant apprentice with his own show who tags along wherever his father performs. At puberty, it is truly something to be ashamed of. And Marvellissimo the Magician and Son are to join John Tapply, the Holy Black and the sexy Silhouettes in the Super Extravaganza Show in the resort hotels on Africa's largest man-made lake this holiday weekend. The non-air conditioned bus grudgingly carries all of them down contoured roads into the Zambezi valley, its engine strained by the mountain inclines and declines and its passenger section cluttered by the band's drum set, the magician's saw-a-woman-in-half-boxes, the egos of the top singers in the country, and cigarette smoke from the lungs of eight loud Silhouettes.

Katie Karbo frowns. 'How old are you? Shouldn't you be in school?'

'Fourteen. Nearly fourteen.' To escape her hot gaze, he looks down at her hands which are folded on the magazine. Her fingernails are purple. On her left ring finger, a diamond sits on a circle of blue stones, held hostage by a circle of pure gold. Her skin is pinched tight around the ring. She holds it to the light of the window. 'He gave it to me last weekend.'

'When are you getting married?'

'Next year. When I finish college.'

She examines her ring from all angles, and then twists it around her finger. 'Why is there no air-conditioning on this bus?'

He stares out of the window again, hoping that her rhetorical question means the end of their conversation. He is too uncomfortably thirteen, afraid his voice will go squeaky, afraid she will notice the beginnings of a moustache on his upper lip. But she insists on violating his private space. 'So what are you going to be when you grow up? A magician?'

He thinks too long before he answers. 'I'm not going to grow up.'

'Me neither. Never.' She slowly lowers an eyelid, as if sealing a secret pact. 'Hey, look, Kariba…'

Kariba is the town that has grown up next to the hydroelectric dam in the Zambezi River basin, and is, after

Victoria Falls, the number one tourist destination in the country, boasting five star hotels, jet skiing, cruises, a blue lake and a white sand beach (sand imported), though the lake is at the bottom of the humid Zambezi valley, seeded by Tsetse fly and malaria. A hundred workers were killed during construction of the dam and the creation of the reservoir forced resettlement of about 57,000 Native Tonga people living along the Zambezi, who until 1955 had lived in a relatively undisturbed paradise of hunting, fishing and gathering. The whites were apparently more concerned with animal life: in 1960 and 1961, 'Operation Noah' captured and removed around 6,000 large animals and numerous small ones threatened by the lake's rising waters, trapped on islands. Dead trees still poke their branches through the shallows of the lake, and hippos and crocodiles sport in its waters.

They are to stay at the Lake View Inn, and perform every night on the large stone floored balcony that overlooks the lake itself – four starry nights of live music, dancing, magic, drama and feasting for local residents and tourists.

Every night Katie and the Silhouettes will perform their routine – dancing in shadow, then in lingerie, then swimwear. There will be no nudity of course, but whoever has choreographed their routines knows what men want – a repetition of all those copulative clichés – pelvic thrusts, shaking breasts, fluttering eyelashes, shuddering orgasm.

The magician's son too is looking forward to the weekend. Performance gives him significance, and an excuse to dress up and camouflage his grey self with the finery of imagination, though he is only a magician. Every night he performs his routine: Clippo, Absorbing News, Torn and Restored Newspaper, Sympathetic Silks, and the inevitable pulling a fake rabbit out of the bulging secret compartment of a top hat. The enthusiastic applause he receives is due, he is sure, not to the skill of his performance, or even the surprise of each trick, or the clever patter he recites, but because he has been billed as the youngest magician in the country. His gawky age has more to do with it than any sleight of hand. The climax of his act is the Sword Box – place the box on assistant's head; thrust the twelve swords through it, after demonstrating that they are real steel; lift the front cover of the box to reveal swords intersecting an empty box with no assistant's head, though she is plainly holding the box with her two hands and sitting demurely in a seat while the swords bisect every conceivable space; rapidly pull the blades out and close the front of the box, then gently lift the box off her head, revealing to incredulous gasps from the audience a smiling, unscathed assistant. Let her curtsey and you bow, holding her hand. How clever. The intact assistant is the hotel manager's daughter, a political move organised by his father so that Mr. Big is smiling from the back row of the audience to watch his darling, and the eleven year old Gail, a blonde Syringa sapling whom he likes but to whom he can only show affection by pushing swords through her head, smiles back.

The Silhouettes begin the show with Abba's 'Dancing Queen', change into itchy grass skirts and coconut bras during his act for the Hawaiian Beach Scene, then slip into silky lingerie during John Tapply's duets with a willowy blonde singer, and after the Mister Marvellissimo, they go neon pink and strobe bikini for Grand Funk Railroad's 'Flight of the Phoenix', twisting pelvises and shaking boobs in an extravaganza of light, sound and limbs.

The magician's son watches and learns. They are showing but not showing, offering then withdrawing their bodies in a sacrifice to some priapic god of lust. But why?

Women, apparently, are commodities to be displayed, bartered, selected, used and discarded. That one. This one. Here are the modern slave traders of Africa. John Tapply: *I like that one; she's got good tits.* Marvellissimo: *She, on the other hand, has a pair of legs on her that goes up to wahoo.*

The only purpose for their dancing, it seems, is to display themselves as sexual objects for sale. But of course they are not for sale. Their commodities have been apportioned into sexual compartments and marketed so as to get maximum profit for minimum value. And as an early apprentice in the female bartering system, there is no choice: his heart has chosen only Katie. He watches her every night on and off stage. He is sold on the way she tosses her hair, the way she smiles into the air, the way she sits afterwards and drinks her gin and tonic at the table, facing the empty blue lake. But he dare not approach her. He is a thirteen-year old boy; she is eighteen; and she is engaged. Her finger glints with the ugly diamond, imprisoning her hand to an adult future. She's booked, it says, bought by some sweaty man in the Capital who wants her all to himself. Even so, she takes the ring off, he notices, for the show each night. It is bad for business – Silhouettes have to look available.

On the second day, while his father is busy preparing props backstage, he slips away and squeezes up courage to sit next to her on the deck of the prostrating blue lake. She looks up; smiles. 'The magician's son. Sit. Sit. Pull up a pew.'

He sits rigidly, swinging his childish, gawky, long legs and not saying anything. But she is not perturbed. She has lots to say in her make-everyone-at-ease, familiar voice. She delivers a smile she uses in the performance. 'How do you do that trick with the magazine?'

'The Vanishing Lady?' He smiles his magician's-oathof-secrecy smile and shrugs shoulders, as he has been taught. 'Can't tell. Would spoil the whole thing.'

'The knives?'

'I really stick them in her head,' he says. 'I've done it so often, she doesn't feel it.'

She punches him on the shoulder with the comradely intimacy of fellow performers. But now she expects him to say something in return.

'How do you do all those dancing routines,' he asks. 'I mean, how do you change costumes so quickly?'

She flutters eyes left, pouts lips left, and her coquettish pony tail bobs on her right shoulder. 'I didn't know you thought about me. What else do you think about me?'

He lets that one slide. 'What does your boyfriend think of you dancing?'

She scratches her chin with a purple nail. 'He's jealous as hell.'

'Let's go for a walk,' she says, when John Tapply pushes his gut out of the lounge and onto the patio. The singer sits heavily at the adjacent table, shadowed by the translucent singer. Katie leans toward her thirteen year old friend in an intimate, hair-tickling frown. 'I can't stand him. He ogles me the whole time. Walks into our dressing room while we're changing.'

John Tapply sports a moustache, sideburns (this is the Seventies, after all) and an ego that announces his presence loudly wherever he walks. You know he is a famous singer by the way he orders his gin and tonic (and Malawi Shandy for the lady, Bwana). Now the magician's son hates him too. Imagine watching her change in and out of those skimpy bikinis. Imagine.

'He stands in our dressing room, as if he's watching a rugby game. On the first night after our first performance' – here she lays a hand on his shoulder, and her breath is sharp and hot on his cheek – 'he walked in while I was topless, and ever since then, he thinks he has the right to make comments and jokes.'

'Topless?'

She spreads her hands as if she is carrying huge naked breasts in them. He is forced to look at her t-shirt with the Lord Kitchener motif (your country wants you), then away at the blue lake, which is suddenly spinning.

They walk together down the spiral staircase; John squints into the sun after them. The path to the lake shore is hot, humid and unpleasant, the green lake weed stinking. The air is still – miniature frothy waves lap at the gritty beach, sharp stones protrude out of the murky water – but she reaches down and pulls off her high heels, and kicks them onto the grassy bank. He slouches off his shoes too, and sloshes water around.

'Is that your girlfriend? Your magical assistant?'

'Gail? No. Gail? She's…' He waves the fairy girl he has pierced with twelve swords every night away. 'She's my father's idea.'

'I envy you,' she says. 'You're… how old?'

'Thir… fourteen, nearly. And you?'

'My life is over. I can see it now. It's a river rushing to the sea. You want to get there, but you don't.'

'A river?' He wades in the warm oily water trying to avoid the sharp stones, watching her legs swirl and her purple-nailed toes wriggle in the mud.

'So she's not your girlfriend.' She scrutinises his burning red face. 'Who is your girlfriend? Do you have one?'

'Yes.' Of course he has a girlfriend, even though he has never talked to her, or been within six feet of her. My girlfriend, he tells her, is Sandra Botticelli. It is a lie. He is a virgin. He is more than a virgin. He is an awkward, gawky

81

half child struggling to break free of his eggshell in full view of the mocking world.

His girlfriend, Sandra Botticelli. His lie sits in the air like a stinking black cloud. She lets it hover. Elton John's piano opening to 'Crocodile Rock' pours over the balcony above them from the hotel's Tempest stereo system and floods its way into their conversation. 'How young is she?'

'Twelve, I think. Thirteen. Well, we're not really…'

'Have you kissed her?'

He has many times in his imagination. But in the last few days, the imaginary girl Sandra, the flat-chested girl from Roosevelt Girls High has been replaced by a more savage image of a full-busted Katie, her lips pouted in challenge.

'You don't have a girlfriend, do you?'

'Why are you asking me that?'

She smiles and, after a quick peek at John's leering hot face over the balcony, takes his face with both hands, pulls it to hers, and presses it flat against her mouth.

Every morning, the performers emerge late from their hotel rooms, eat breakfast, lie on the deck, or drive over to Caribbean Bay, a hotel that boasts a white sand beach, the only fifty foot stretch of beach in this landlocked country, where you pay $3 to get in and you lie and bake in the hot sun, the feeble waves of the lake lapping at the edges – Kariba weed cleared, crocodiles banished by nets, a Greek style terrace overlooking the water, waiter to hover over you with 75c Malawi Shandies. This morning, she invites him over to the beach to 'get away from John'. His father is preoccupied with rehearsing his sawing a woman in half act, which nearly failed the previous night, and the blonde woman has graciously volunteered to lie in the wooden coffin while he saws through her stomach, so the magician's son escapes for the morning. The hotel bus steals them away, and his father seems only too glad to be left alone with his giggling assistant. Soon he and Katie are sipping iced shandies in the sand, on a rock-sheltered inlet. She lies back on the towel, sunglasses over closed eyes, coconut suntan glistening on her flesh, shaved armpits sweating as she rests her head on her hands. He cannot help looking at her breasts flattening and spilling out the sides of her pink bikini top. But when her eyelashes twitch, he knows he has been caught, and turns away, ashamed. He hunches forward, draws a circle in the sand with his toe.

She smiles up at the blue sky. 'They're actually a nuisance, they're so big.'

He cannot believe she is talking about the unmentionables. He measures the horizon between dead trees that poke out of the skin of the lake.

'Since I started taking the pill, they just grew out of shape. They used to be so perfect. You should have seen them. Now they're just balloons. Stretch marks. They sag. They don't tell you that when you go on the pill.'

All he can do is echo her last words, like a concave valley of dead rock. 'The pill?'

He has, of course, blotted out the fact that she has sex regularly with a sweaty, adult male, a boyfriend, a suitor, a fiancé, as she calls him. But aren't they supposed to wait until they are married? Isn't she supposed to be a virgin bride offered up to the male god, sacrificing herself to be impaled on a sword and then thrown into the everlasting torment of adulthood?

'Do you mind if I go topless?' With a furtive look at the rocks and cliffs, she flips down her bikini top and lies down again, her white breasts now exposed to the unforgiving sunlight. He lies back, as she does, and tries to stare up at the sky. The sun is too hot, but the sound of lapping dead trees drowning in the shallows hides his silence, and a hot breeze fans his embarrassment. But when he closes his eyes, he cannot avoid reproducing that first fleeting glance he has had: white balloons, plugged by nipples; around each nipple, a circle of holes, as if they have been stitched on; stretch marks, as if a tiger has mauled her, and blue veins radiating from the red eyes.

'Derek would kill me. He…'

'Derek?'

'My fiancé.'

That kills any desire for the moment. In fact there is no desire present anyway, only a nervous gratitude that she has revealed to him what she has hidden from all those men. The magician's son is a privileged initiate into the Goddess cult.

He murmurs sympathy. 'No, they're nice.'

'Thank you.'

He sits up again, careful not to stare, and skims a stone across the muddy surface of the lake, but the water hyacinth stops it dead after one bounce. He stares at the cumulonimbus clouds mushrooming against the horizon, watching them grow cancerously out of shape in the heat, his bruised purple feelings ready to flicker and thunder and rain. But behind him, the sand crunches, and ice in glasses tinkle to warn him that they are no longer alone.

'Hello, hello.' John Tapply and his assistant wave margueritas at the two sun worshippers.

'Oh, shit.' Katie slips her bikini top up so that her breasts are again the mysterious desire of all men.

He is glad to return to the comforting arms of his role as magician that night. His father's new assistant, the blonde woman, sports a mini skirt, a bee-hive hairdo and a high giggle, which she reproduces every time his patter demands it: *This is one of those tricks you can do better in the dark – I bet you know one or two tricks that you can do better in the dark* (giggle). *After I saw you in half, you'll be able to lead a double life* (giggle). The magician's son faithfully reproduces his father's skill, but not his easy manner with assistants, and can barely acknowledge Gail as she curtsies and submits primly to his twelve swords. After his show, instead of chatting breezily with her at the bar, as his father does to his assistant, or sliding his hand up her leg, as his father does to his assistant, or disappearing with her out in the dark night, he sits crouched in the wings, watching the Silhouettes, or 'fancy ladies' as Gail contemptuously calls them.

He is still fascinated with the ritual of these semi-naked girls dancing at leering red faced, beer-bellied, receding-hairlined, office men who drink beer and cheer and jeer. But he is no more an observer – that night, the magician's son bites into his pain as Katie Karbo skewers his heart with twelve knives. He tries to console himself with the thought that he knows her secret; he knows what the others don't know – she can flaunt her breasts all she wants, but he knows her secret: they have stretch marks, they are big and cumbersome, they are a burden to her, the nipples are sullen plugs. But this does little to soothe the black ruffled waters inside him.

After the penultimate performance, she beckons him onto the deck. The moonlight cools the hot black sky, and crickets screech in the black bushes. They sweat outside on the garden chairs facing the dark unconsciousness of Lake Kariba. The other silhouettes perch their mini skirted bottoms on high stools in the bar, smoke, drink and flirt, while the band plays for the dancing audience in the open lounge. Katie drinks wine, pointing the glass at him after every swig. She has something to tell him.

'You don't drink?' she says. 'No, of course you don't, you're only fourteen bloody years old.'

He measures the silence with twenty beats of his pounding heart.

'You know that you can ask me to do anything you want,' she says.

He scratches his upper lip, and clears his throat. He swings his legs violently under the table until they collide with her shin.

'You're cute,' she says. 'You could ask anything and I would do it.'

He swallows. 'Thank you.'

'Ask me something,' she says. 'What do you want me to do?'

He doesn't know what he wants her to do. What does he want from her? He can't know.

'You're so young, dammit. You don't want to marry me or want me to be anything.'

'No,' he says.

'So what do you want? You never say anything. Do you like me?' She tickles his spotty chin, fingers his upper lip. His face burns red and loud.

'Do you know what I want to do with you?' she says.

'No.'

'Come, let's walk.' Elton John's 'Yellow Brick Road' (or another song) echoes over the balcony while they walk. She is a foot taller than him, and he strings along beside her. They walk through a dark pathway to the boat launch. A canoe laps on the dark water, tethered by a rope to a gnarled tree stump.

'Are we safe here?' she says.

He thinks of hippos, though he knows this is not what she means. He can't see any hippos, and has never seen any, but the picture is as vivid as if they are before him: floating backwards with eyes protruding, contemptuous snorts to warn them. He thinks too of crocodiles. They pull you into the water and drown you in the dark before they eat you, his father has told him. She picks her way through choking hyacinth foaming on the black surface of a lake where once trees grew and tribes fished. The two of them reach a concrete dock.

Then they are in the canoe; she unties the rope and sets them adrift; he paddles hard to free them from the weeds, and they glide across the bay. They are in the safe zone – no crocodiles ripple the waters here, or hippos who can (his father has told him) bite a canoe in two.

'Enough.' The canoe jiggles when she huddles closer to him, and black water laps over the edge when she helps him lay the paddles to rest. 'Do you know why I dance?'

He shakes his head. She is holding both his hands tight.

'I dance to get away from myself, from him, from this' – she points her engagement ring at him.

'Do you love him?'

'Of course I do. Of course. It's not that; it's the inevitability of the whole thing. You live, you marry, you have kids, you die. And you meet you. I mean I meet you, and you're so young, but you're the one I want because I can't; you're outside of the whole thing.'

They watch the Lake View Inn terrace twinkle with lights. Crocodile Rock echoes half a mile across a black chasm.

She presses her arms on his shoulders, leans against him, her head on his shoulder. The crickets in his ears pulse louder than the Elton John song that weaves in and out of the wind.

She has planned it this way, she is ashamed to say: a canoe ride is the only way to get away from John Tapply. His moustache tickles her when he kisses her, she says.

Tapply wants her so badly, baby. But she wants him – you – the magician's son. The dark Lady of the Lake is a Katie no one else has seen, she says, a regretful, wistful, fourteen year old girl inside the woman's body.

Do you know what happens to the wild spirits of children when they grow up? she asks. They are imprisoned in flesh, in breasts, in bras, in adult prisons, in rings of obligation and behaviour. Whereas, she claims, he is free. Free, you understand? Free.

The canoe drifts under the willows and the dead corpses of blackened trees; a night bird explodes into the sky and into the underworld beyond. The distant sound of the party – a laugh, the music, the tinkle of a broken glass – comes muted, behind a thick glass plate, and the heavy sky is a shroud thrown over them. He feels her pressing on him for support, for admiration, for solace, for what? Something he cannot give. He wriggles backward.

The canoe tips. She screams as she falls in, and he is sucked under too as she grabs onto him: she wrestles with him, laughing, her sodden clothing tangling and suffocating him, her flailing limbs feigning helplessness. He cannot pull her up onto the canoe. In the dark glue of the water, she holds him tight and presses her legs against him as she drags him under, her arms tightening, while he gasps for buoyancy, the black liquid and the smell of her hyacinth hair flapping against him.

He finally tips the canoe right side up with super human strength and they drape their arms over it to catch their breath. He hopes someone will save him. Not his father. John Tapply swimming strongly, grimly through the water: Hey, what the hell do you think you're doing? John at the side of the canoe, rescuing them. Or better – hippos snorting in lust at finding them, crunching the canoe in half. Or a crocodile. We'd better get out of here, he says. He paddles, while she laughs, fearless, ready for death. Did anyone hear us besides the hippos? Oh God, my God. What am I doing? You're a child.

The last performance is a climax of sorts, dancing, magic, music, encored by the Holy Black and John Tapply singing, the Silhouettes gyrating to *Flight of the Phoenix*, and Katie's blue eyes hot on him all evening. They share a secret, the shame of something black and deep that is drowning him still.

The journey back to the capital is clammy and uncomfortable. Katie sits with her Silhouette friends, filling up the dark silence of his presence with trills of laughter and whispers in other ears, and after three hours of ascent into the civilised world, they are home. The bus stop at the Monomatapa Hotel is shrouded by a pack of heavy set men with hairy arms claiming their baggage as it arrives, holding hands, hugging, kissing. The magician's son peers through the bus window as Katie's man lifts her up with one arm and kisses her roughly so his beard grinds into her soft flesh.

'God, I missed you, darling.'

'Me too,' she says. The magician's son climbs down, watches her as she laughs loud, aware of him watching, her fiancé the ugliest man he has ever seen. She turns once, finally, and nods goodbye. He nods back and her boyfriend quizzes her with a who-the-hell-is-that look. Oh, just some boy, the magician's son, he can do magic too, sort of thing, ha ha...

He is watching her go to her death; she knows it too. And he has been ripped apart by some creature from hell trying to clutch onto him as she fell into the dark waters, but he is still here, alive and – she is right – free. He loves her now, pities her mostly, but loves her too. If he were older, or if she were the twelve year old crush of his, or if he were that hulk of a fiancé, maybe it could have been, but... no: it is better to leave it in the realm of the impossible, and leave her – the dark, lake goddess – in her restless torture.

'Did you have a good time this weekend?' his father asks him. 'Look, there's your mother.'

Green Island

Tuesday, 24 October. Baghdad shimmered in heat haze. Abrahem parked the car, a metallic blue Volvo, at the top end of Al-Rashid Street. He looked at his kids, Amira aged nine and Mohammed aged five, in the back seat.

'Stay in the car and lock the doors. Speak to no one. I won't be long.'

Going to the bank meant shaking hands with many people, sitting sometimes to drink coffee with the bank manager (Abrahem's uncle was a wealthy businessman, had many friends), and waiting patiently in long lines. Amira and Mohammed played a game in the hot car – he could see them clapping hands and counting as he walked off.

On his return, Abrahem waved to his children. He reached for the keys in his pocket. They clambered to the window, opened it. 'Baba, do you have any sweets for us?'

Two metres away from his car, the bomb exploded.

The fireball threw him back onto the pavement. He saw the car shatter and fly in pieces into the sky. He heard screaming. Maybe it came from his own mouth. He saw people running in the smoke, and he found himself lying on the hard concrete amidst rubble. Then he saw that his arms were pierced with a hundred pieces of concrete and metal. His shirt ripped. Blood seeped from what looked like a thousand knife wounds. But he was all right. He could feel no pain. He could stand. He could shout. He didn't care about himself. He ran towards the mangled wreckage of his car. He could see two bodies. They both lay still, one in the frame of the wrecked car, the other on the pavement, thrown wide through the window. No screaming, no crying. He fought his way through the flames and heat – a passer-by tried to hold him back – and saw the blood. He went for his daughter first. She lay face down, her brown hair gleaming in the sun.

An arm. A leg. A head surrounded by a bloody halo.

She felt heavier in his arms than she had ever been alive. The weight in his heart was such that he could hardly stand. 'Please God. Help us.'

He laid Amira on his jacket, listened for her heart. The ground rumbled. His own heart beat in his ears. She made no sound.

He reached into the car and pulled Mohammed from the backseat. His child, torn in a thousand places. 'He's alive! Quick, the ambulance.' He reached for his mobile phone, but his trousers were in shreds and the pockets were gone.

A crowd gathered: some talked on phones, others took pictures like tourists. 'No,' he shouted. Mobile phones have been known to detonate second explosions when a crowd gathers to help with the first.

His own phone had been thrown onto the far pavement. A stranger picked it up and saw a message. He pressed redial and Abrahem's wife answered it. 'Who is this?' The man said: 'There's been a bomb. Your husband and your two children are dead.' When he heard the screaming at the other end, he threw the phone down again on the pavement.

Abrahem heard the ambulance siren long before it arrived. And then he was scooped up in the strong arms of a medic. 'You sit in the back, old man.'

Abrahem was not an old man. He was thirty-six. But today he moved like an old man, and his brain was befuddled. He had lost most of his words. All he could say was: 'My son, my daughter.'

'Your boy is in critical condition, old man. He may not live. We will do our best.'

'Amira?'

The medic shook his head.

'A phone, I need a phone…'

He got through to his uncle. They were closer than brothers. 'I'm at Ibn Al Bitar Hospital. Tell my wife.'

There was no mystery. Abrahem was a policeman, and Al Qaeda didn't like policemen co-operating with the American occupiers or the puppet government. The bomb was a message. But he had been a policeman long before the fall of Saddam – it was his career, his livelihood. For fifteen years he had been a policeman, dealing with petty crime and family disputes. He had juggled compromises and taken into account human foibles. He had been a good policeman – corruptible, conscientious, compassionate. There was no other way here. Although Iraq was the first place on earth to have the written rule of law, this was not how business could be done these days.

On his mantelpiece at home stood a photo of himself with his arms around a US soldier at the beginning of the occupation, when they were all heroes together. He was smiling, showing the world the V sign for peace.

The hospital treated him for minor lacerations and then discharged him. They kept his son in intensive care with a drip in his arm, a bandage around his head, and his arm in a sling. His daughter was buried at a quiet funeral so as not to attract attention. Every day after work, he maintained a vigil at the hospital, watching his son. His uncle too spent the evenings with him.

Was he angry? Did he want revenge? No. He was defeated. Sadness overwhelmed him. The lead skies fell down that day and buried his girl in the rubble.

He had nightmares. Every night, his wife would wake him gently. 'You were shouting.'

He watched his son heal, went to the hospital every

night for three months. His uncle, a faithful friend, sat by his son's bedside, and they talked, to while away the night hours.

The wounds began to heal. His son was covered in deep purple scabs. Don't pick at them Mohammed. Don't pick. They're itchy because they're healing.

'It's a miracle, this healing,' said his uncle. 'A miracle.'

But one day at the hospital, his uncle did not show up. Abrahem called home, and listened to his wife crying.

'He's been kidnapped.'

Sure enough, that night, a cold voice on the other end of the phone said: 'We're going to kill your uncle.'

'What has he done? He has done nothing.'

'We want a hundred thousand US. By Friday. Bring it to the place we tell you.'

'I don't have a hundred thousand.'

'Your uncle does. He's a business man. Go to the bank and talk to them.'

Every morning at six, they'd phone and harass him for the money. Meanwhile he would hold his son who was healing. A brave boy. Stop picking at those scars, Mohammed.

He had to get the hundred thousand. His uncle had a secret bank account, one Abrahem had access to for emergencies.

It made his heart constrict, if that's what this tightening of the chest was, this painful thumping. They must have tortured him, Abrahem thought. They must have gouged this secret truth out of him with a knife. His uncle would never have told them otherwise. One hundred thousand US dollars was the exact amount his uncle had stashed away. He tried not to think about what they had done, what they were doing, what they would do to his uncle. He had heard the stories. He knew people who knew people who had

94

fallen into their hands. This tightening of the skin, this restricting of the larynx, these cold sweaty palms told him his life was not going to be good. And that there were no secrets anymore. No secrets.

He forged his uncle's signature, used his pin, as they had planned for such an emergency, and withdrew as much money as he could – five thousand.

His wife caught him thumbing through the grubby pile, and then pressing it behind the tins at the back of the cupboard. 'You're not going to give them the money.'

He ignored her.

'It's a trap. They want you, and when they have you, they'll kill you and your uncle and take the money too. Go to the police.'

'I am the police.'

So she brought in reinforcements. His friends sat around him on the veranda after supper, sucked on their cigarettes, and talked into the smoke. 'Don't go, Abrahem. Where do they want you to take the money, anyway?'

'Sadr City.'

'They'll shoot you in the head. You know Sadr City. It's where they execute people. Haven't you watched them on YouTube?'

'What are you telling me? That I must let my uncle die?'

'Yes. Leave the country before they kill you and your family. Leave your uncle. He's an old man. He's lived enough.'

'Get out.' Abrahem stood. 'I didn't invite you here to insult my uncle.'

'Abrahem, please... You asked for our advice. Listen to your friends.'

'My uncle saved my life many times. I love my uncle.'

'If you asked your uncle now, he would tell you the

same. He would say – save your family. Save yourself. Leave the country while you still can.'

'There must be another way. Maybe I could talk with them. Reason with them.'

'They speak with bullets and bombs, Abrahem.'

They talked long into the night. Abrahem postponed sleep as long as possible. And when he did sleep, the nightmares jabbed him awake. Always the same – a shot to the temple, the weight of his daughter's body. He leaped out of bed, still hearing the echo of the shot in his head, still feeling the weight of the ceiling pressing down on him.

If he went, he would surely die. And his uncle too. The money would be gone. All the money his uncle had saved.

His boy healed rapidly. He could walk now, and move his right arm. He wore the bandage around his head like a crown.

Abrahem removed more and more of the money from the bank that week. He took pocketfuls to the Souq and waved it in the money changers' faces, shouting out 'U.S., U.S., U.S.'

It made quite a pile in the kitchen cabinet. He hadn't realised how much money one hundred thousand U.S. dollars actually was. It could serve them well. They could flee the country, go to a stable country (like Syria,) start a new life. They would be OK.

So said his friends, his tempters, the so-called 'wise' old men. But he knew he could never do it. He would be haunted by his uncle's death; he would die with the guilt and shame. He may as well take a gun to his uncle's head himself and shoot.

Every day, he went back to the bank where his daughter had been killed. And every day he changed the money at the Souq, waving fistfuls of dirty notes, and the money changers replacing them with crisp neat piles of greenbacks.

They watched him, he knew; their eyes spied on him everywhere; they knew his every move. He lived these days like a rat in a cage.

When he could not bear the pain any more, he made a decision. He would take them the money, plead for his uncle's life, and his life, and for the life of his family. And once he had decided on a path, he felt happier. See, he said to the hidden eyes watching him from dark alleyways, see, I am doing what you want me to do.

If they killed him, if they killed his uncle, his wife and son would have to flee. But where could a woman go on her own? She would have to return to her relatives in the South. And for this she needed money. So he made a contingency plan: the money stashed in the kitchen was for his wife and son. He would go with a few thousand to the kidnappers, plead for more time to get the rest. The promise of the remainder of the money would keep him and his uncle alive. He would buy time. Meanwhile, he would talk to them – reason with them.

This is when Abrahem had the Dream. Not the usual nightmare, but a peaceful vision of a green island where the waves frothed onto the golden shores, where the palm trees were ripe with coconuts, and dates hung heavy over him, within easy reach. Servants offered him cool drinks in the shade of a leaning loquat tree. The land breathed quietly, the sea sparkled deep blue. And in the dream his son and daughter played on the beach, laughing, clapping hands.

He had never seen a place like this. He had always lived land-locked in Baghdad; he had been to the grey, churning sea only once, but Al-Basra was a hellish body of water, sticky and hot, choked with litter and dead fish.

The dream, a vision of paradise, called him home, its recurring vivid tangibility a sign that he was surely going to die.

Friday morning, the bank was closed and he had only twenty five thousand dollars. The phone call came at six promptly. He appealed for mercy. He suggested an instalment plan.

He heard men arguing in the background.

'I can't withdraw more than five thousand a day, you know that...'

The voice was calm. 'OK. Bring the money today after Friday prayers. You can get the rest later. But we want all of it, and only then he goes free. Maybe.'

His wife did not speak to him as she prepared breakfast. She chopped and peeled and fried. She banged pots, slammed cupboards.

As he had no car, he hailed a yellow and black taxi and directed the driver where to go. He could see the whites in the man's eyes as they approached the area. At the roadblock, he nodded. 'This is OK.'

He picked his way through the rubble of the suburb that had been left untouched since the 2008 siege of Sadr City.

The building loomed ahead. He knew they were watching; he thought once he caught sight of the muzzle of an AK. If I die, I will die with a clear conscience.

The building smelt musty with the fear of all who had passed through here before him. He took measured breaths.

The green island appeared before him, a shimmering mirage, something he could almost smell.

He put one foot ahead of the other, slapping each shoe down to show them he was here. No point in sneaking around. Show them he was not afraid. At a doorway, an arm beckoned and as soon as he poked his head inside, strong arms gripped him around the throat and pulled him into the darkness. They frisked him for weapons. He lifted his arms, let them poke and feel and tear. Satisfied, the arms steered him to a chair in the middle of the room. Although he could see nothing in the dark – sacking covered the windows – he could swear he recognised the room from all those executions on the Internet, from all those grainy clips on Al-Jazeera – masked men, banners behind them on all the walls. But as he adjusted to the dark room, he saw these walls were bare, black with a thousand fingerprints. And speckled white and red spots dripped like porridge on one spot of the wall opposite him. Three dark figures paced the shadows like tigers in a cage.

'The money.'

He recognised the voice on the phone. He pulled the notes out of the lining of his jacket in tufts and spread them on the table in front of him. 'My uncle?'

As his eyes grew more accustomed to the light, he saw them. Young men with scarce beards. No masks, no face covering, just jeans and t-shirts. American clothes, he wanted to say to them. You who hate Americans are wearing their clothes. They each held an AK 47. No one needed to tell him that this was a bad sign. They only showed people who they were if they were going to kill them. A young man paced up and down the room, playing with the safety catch of his weapon. Two others spoke in whispers. They had a mission. He wondered which one had planted the bomb that had killed his daughter.

'Not even twenty thousand, old man. What are you trying to do here?'

'There's twenty five thousand. I'll get the rest. Where is my uncle?'

The leader of the group stirred the greenbacks with his rifle muzzle. They had not pointed their weapons at him – a good sign. He looked at each man, appealed with his eyes.

'My uncle?'

The leader he had identified as the older man gave a nod, and the young man opened the door to an internal room. Seconds later, they hauled a body through the door, bound, gagged, doubled up, the whites of his eyes all Abrahem could see. Alive.

'He's OK?' Abrahem half-stood but the man behind him pressed the muzzle of a hot AK into his temple.

'If you kill us, we cannot get the money.'

He should not have spoken. The arm yanked his head back so that he stared into the dead metal barrel of the rifle. 'You think we want money, you think this is what it is all about? Who do you think we are?'

'You tell him, old man.'

The older man pulled off the filthy rag. His uncle's lips were cracked, his nose bleeding. Abrahem could see he had not had any water or food. 'You have to stop supporting the regime,' his uncle said to the floor. 'They watch you go to work every day. They want you to stop.'

'We've been watching you,' said the man behind Abrahem. 'And we don't like what we see.'

'You have to stop. And because you don't stop, because you don't listen, we will have to stop you.'

The young man stepped forward and cocked his weapon. He stood with feet apart, balancing himself.

Abrahem's mouth dried. He wanted to talk, but the words vanished. He opened his mouth to speak, and the words came from his uncle's lips.

'What will his wife do?' said his Uncle. 'What will she do if he is dead? She can't be left alone. She's a woman on her own. She can't be left alone without a man.'

'Where is her father?' said the older man. 'Her family?'

Abrahem shook his head.

'At the beginning of the occupation,' said his uncle. 'They died in the bombing raids. The Americans killed them.'

The older man chewed on his cigarette. A good answer.

'Allah is merciful,' said his uncle. 'To those who obey his laws. And it is against his laws to widow women.'

'Who are you to tell us the law?' The young man whisked the AK around to point at his uncle. But the older man held up his hand. He gave a slight turn of his head and walked out of the inner door. The other boys followed him. Abrahem heard whispering, heard the younger man scuffing his boot against the floorboards.

His uncle winked at him. He nodded back. He was sweating. Keep calm, he told himself. Keep the tsunami of fear back, back, back. Hold it in.

And then the door opened. They held their AK's at port. The young man held his weapon stiff. The older man untied his uncle. He had been bound in a foetal position for days so he could hardly stand when he was released. Abrahem had to help him up, though he could hardly stand on his own shimmering legs. The older man opened the outer door.

'Go,' he said.

Leaning on each other, they stumbled out into the passageway and down the concrete steps. His uncle was heavy. Heavy like death. He remembered the shape of his daughter's heaviness. He placed one foot in front of the other. That's how his life would be now, a placing of one step in front of the other.

The entrance was a blinding green flash of light in his eyes. Green as the island in his dream. He heard his daughter laughing But then the darkness behind him choked the vision. He dared not turn around – he could feel the cold hand of a black shadow on his shoulder. They could still shoot: it had happened before. Either they change their mind or the young one decides to do what he wanted to do, or else it's their plan all along, to execute them this way.

The light at the entrance blinded him. Every step. His

uncle pushed through first, and then he squeezed through. His back was covered with spiders of fear.

Out on the street, they were not safe yet. The men watched from the window above, trained snipers. No leaping or running or anything that would change the delicate hair trigger of their wills. Even when he began crying, his uncle jabbed him in the ribs. 'No, no,' he hissed. 'No.'

And then they were at the roadblock and past it, and in a taxi and driving at breakneck speed, their windows open, their bodies shaking as they held each other tightly. They said nothing: there was nothing to be said. The only way Abrahem could show gratitude was by clenching his uncle's hand.

At home, over supper and a smoke, he tried to express his gratitude in words. But the words were heavy, slow in coming.

His uncle shook his head. 'I made them a deal.'

'What deal?'

His uncle shook his head again. 'You must leave the country. You and Hiba and Mohammed. And you must take the money with you.'

'What about you?'

His uncle shook his head.

'I'm not going without you.'

'They'll come after you. That's your part of the deal. Either you leave the country, or they kill you.'

'And you?'

'I'll be OK. I made a deal with them. If you go, I'll be safe.'

The journey to Syria smoothed out easier than anticipated. The money helped. A few folded greenbacks in the passports worked magic. They headed straight to the United

Nations refugee centre in Dimashqa and stared up at the blue UNHCR sign while the guard searched them. Inside, they waited in queues, squatted on floors awash with crying babies and women with dead eyes, and finally someone ushered them into a sterile office.

On the walls of the office hung pictures of smiling brown faces in clean, bright cities. Al-Qaeda was a word that attracted sympathy and understanding from the white faces. His record as a policeman too helped. But what helped the most was the photo of Amira smiling at the camera in her bright t-shirt, against the backdrop of her father hosing down the Volvo in his driveway.

A Pakistani man typed up the paperwork in triplicate on a manual Olivetti typewriter. Dozens of photos were stamped and stapled to the forms, and greenbacks were passed from palm to palm to expedite the process.

They waited in a hotel. One week passed. Two weeks. Three weeks.

Finally, a white, bright man in uniform called them into his office. 'Two countries have offered you asylum. Canada and Australia.'

Abrahem went blank. 'You mean we can choose?'

He had never given one thought to Australia or Canada, ever. He didn't even know where they were. Two Western countries where no one spoke Arabic were of no interest to him whatsoever. But now, they were magic words that gleamed with effervescent light.

'You can apply... But look at what each offers first.' He handed Abrahem forms, and more forms, all in tiny hieroglyphics, in writing that sloped backward. He piled him high with brochures of glossy smiling faces against beautiful landscapes.

'They set you up with some money, accommodation, free medical facilities... until you can find your feet.'

103

Outside again, Pakistani translators pocketed their greenback gifts and read out the forms. They also offered free advice. 'Take Canada. There are many of us there.'

'Canada is a vast icy wasteland,' said another. Your soul will go grey and die there…'

'But Australia is just a big desert.'

'Australia is just a big island in the middle of nowhere. You'll never see family again.'

The brochures made it feel like a holiday they were planning. They stared at snowy mountains, red deserts, glass cities and sparkling beaches.

'Wait,' said Abrahem. 'Where is that?'

'Somewhere in Queensland, Australia.'

Abrahem let his fingers slowly spread over the glossy page. He could almost hear the waves crashing, the laughter of children. Green water shimmered, and palm trees rustled as they bowed low to the water, ripe with fruit.

Promise Me This

'Promise me this, Josh,' said my father, 'when I die, don't give me a Catholic funeral. I don't want that priest up there' – he pointed to the steeple visible in the white English sky through the living room window of his bungalow – 'muttering his mumbo-jumbo, hocus-pocus over my dead body.'

I promised.

'I don't want him to set foot in the house, understand?'

'I promise, Dad.'

The aggressive prostate cancer had spread into his bones. The doctor had given him a year to live, tops.

I visited as often as I could. Coltishall, on the Norfolk broads, is a long way from the East Coast of Australia. That summer, I found him cheerily philosophical about his own demise. I took him to the hospital for blood plasma, for tests, and I sorted out his pill regime. He spoke about his great awakening out of the slumber of Church tyranny. He was on a quest, he told me, for the truth. In this final year of his life, he would get to the bottom of it. All of it.

Our daily discussions burned with urgent intensity. I learned that he had finally torn away the façade of his life, the guilt and fear of his upbringing, and had come to an understanding of the falsity of all religion, especially this 'whore of Babylon', the Holy Roman Catholic and Apostolic Church. His youth had been stolen from him in the Forties by sadistic priests at his Catholic school; he had quietly suffered sexual repression and denial his entire adult life; but now, at seventy five years old, he was finally enlightened. It started with *The Da Vinci Code* and its ancillary texts: *The Chalice and The Blade,* and *Holy Blood, Holy Grail.* Christ had been demystified.

His eyes were now open. He pronounced himself a secular rationalist.

'You have to do something, Josh,' hissed my aunt at the obligatory family gathering in their back garden. 'Stop him.' She pointed to my father standing by the tea table, surrounded by a crowd of bemused relatives. Children screamed around them, playing British Bulldog.

I could hear, even at this distance that he was railing against the Church. He did little else. 'It's all made up,' he said, within earshot of the children. 'I mean, John, do you seriously believe that that man up there...' He pointed up at the spire in the sky, where white doves cooed and flapped their wings '...can mumble a few words over a piece of bread and a glass of wine and turn them into the body and blood of a man who died two thousand years ago? Do you? Do you?'

My uncle shook his head. 'Perhaps now is not the time to talk about it, Mike.'

'Then when? After I'm dead?'

'The children...'

'In front of the children,' hissed my aunt. 'We all agree with him, but you don't tell children that Santa Claus doesn't exist, do you?'

Her job, my aunt told me, was to hold everything together. This family has been built on tradition, she said. 'You went off to Australia – maybe you don't understand that. Your father is pulling the family apart. I'll be damned if I let that happen.'

We presented ourselves as a good Catholic family. My well-off uncle and aunt were prominent philanthropists, served on prominent committees, well thought of in the higher echelons of East Anglian society. Hundreds of years ago, this family had been persecuted for its faith. And everyone, generations of frail grannies and screaming infants, went to Mass every Sunday.

'I'll try.'

But what of the extracted promise and the loyalty to his quest for truth?

The priest of the parish, often present at family gatherings, was an example not of the ferocity or the intolerance of the Church, but of the pathetic weakness of its power today in secular British Society. He smelled of wool and sour milk, wore sandals with socks, smiled much too often, and had far too many teeth in his mouth. I took him as an unfortunate cliché, and it seemed unfair of my father to rant and rave against this harmless man, who proclaimed a soapy love for all mankind, pressing clean hands on children's heads, and lisped, which kept all the children entertained through those long church services: *On the night he was betwayed, Chwist bwoke the bwead...*

My father, to be fair, demonstrated more tolerance of human frailty that I did; he stood against the monster of the Church itself. He built his arsenal with reason, argument and a foundation of scientific rationalism, and pitied this delusional creature of a parish priest.

When he discovered my father was terminally ill that same summer, the priest beckoned me after church, and asked if he could visit.

'Er... not at this time, Father. He's going through some difficult issues.'

'Death is always a difficult issue. Coming to terms with your Maker's weckoning is always a difficult issue.'

'Yes.' But of course my father now firmly believed – and proclaimed it loudly to the family – that there was no life after death. 'You live on in your children, in the memories of others, in your family's love, in your stories, Josh, if you ever write about me after I'm gone.' There is no such thing as the soul, he said. 'And the idea that you go to lie in the arms of Jesus merely because a toothy, lisping man with soapy hands sprinkles your coffin with Holy Water is bloody preposterous.'

My mother, a good believer, with her unquestioning childlike faith, bustled around the house, banging things, sighing to herself all summer. Religion was not to be torn apart like this, she told me. And my aunt, who had come to discuss funeral arrangements, whispered to her in the kitchen. 'What can we do with this man?'

'At my funeral,' my father said to aunt and uncle, while my mother poured tea and clanked spoons, 'I want no hymns, no prayers, and no priest. If you want, you can read Galileo's words – *E pur si muove*! And Josh has already agreed to recite Dylan Thomas's 'Do not Go Gentle into that Dark Night'.'

'But Mike...'

'Old age should burn and rave at close of day,' my father said. 'Rage, rage against the dying of the light.'

'Father Paddy will conduct the service, of course... we have to have a religious...'

My father shook his head. 'Religion? Best business in town; biggest con in history.'

And that was the end of it.

I returned for a bleak and icy Christmas to find an emaciated and ailing father who couldn't walk, and who apologised for his frailty. 'It's got me, Josh. Don't I look awful? It's in the bones now.'

The regime of pills was giving him alternative constipation and diarrhoea, the targeted radiotherapy on his thigh and ribs made him nauseous, but he kept up his good spirits. He still read ferociously. 'A good book is all I need. A good clear mind is what I'm grateful for.'

Aunt and Uncle whispered in my ear at Christmas lunch and the Boxing Day party. 'Reason with him, Josh. Father

Paddy wants to see him. At least get him to come to Mass.'

But to no avail. His convictions were strong. 'Promise me, promise me, Josh.'

'I promise.'

No chance then of a Catholic funeral. A dying man on a cross? All invented clap-trap. The Nicene Creed? He refused to say it. He'd been lying all his life, but now he had blown away the chaff, widened the cracks, pulled apart and exposed the Church for the sham it was. It had oppressed mankind for centuries. Not anymore. Not this man.

At Easter, I made yet another torturous journey from Brisbane to Singapore to Heathrow, to Norwich, to Coltishall, and found him dying. He had thinned into an emaciated ghost of himself, and our home had been turned into a hospital ward. A drip fed intravenous morphine into his arm, and cheerful nurses turned and bed-panned and fed him through a straw, riding vigil at his side, day and night.

He could not see properly. Could not read. And to my consternation, by his bedside that evening crouched none other than Father Paddy, administering Holy Communion. *After the night he was betwayed, Chwist bwoke bwead... and he gave it to his disciples, saying, dwink, this is my blood...*

'Join us, Josh,' said my mother.

'But Dad...' I said after the priest had left.

'A good man,' said my father. 'I don't believe in all the stuff, but nor does he – he quietly forgets it.'

Father Paddy visited every day, a calm hand on my head, soapy fingers at our lips with the host, *the body of chwist.*

I brought the good news that I was teaching *The Da Vinci Code* at university that semester. 'I used all your notes, Dad, all your sources, for our *Popular Novels* course. It's a hit.'

He waved this news away. 'Destructive, all that stuff,' he said. 'Where's the love of Christ in all that, Josh?'

'I...'

'We don't worry about that clap-trap anymore,' he said. My mother smiled at his bedside, held his hand.

And Father Paddy, more and more omnipresent at our house, gave his toothy grin.

'The funeral arrangements?'

'Oh, your aunt and uncle have sorted that all out with Father Paddy here.'

When you're dying, who knows what pressures you are under? Were the drugs befuddling him into submission, into a benevolent fuzziness with family and priest? I didn't know.

'But you still want the Dylan Thomas, right?'

My father frowned into the distant past. 'Dylan Thomas?'

The nurses came and went, Father Paddy came and went, and I stayed by his side, brushed his lips with a sponge on a stick to ease the terrible thirst when he couldn't eat or drink anymore. 'That nurse kissed me on the lips,' my father told me with his grey, unseeing eyes.

The priest was there to the end. He prayed over him; he watched him as my father took his last breath. 'See you in heaven, Mike, at the right hand of Jesus.' My mother held his cold hand, and I stared through blurry eyes.

The funeral was a magnificent affair. All the family turned up, all sixty relatives, all good Catholics, and the children sat beautifully frocked and suited in the front rows, staring at the shiny coffin wreathed with flowers and a golden cross with a bronze Christ nailed to it. We sang the rousing hymns – favourites of the family – and Father Paddy read from John chapter eleven: *And Jesus cwied in a loud voice – Awise! Awise! Lazawus, come forth. And he that was dead came forth…*

The sermon assured us that Mike smiled down at us from heaven: 'He was a good Catholic. He lived a good Catholic life. His unwavering faith and his good deeds ensure him a place at the right hand of God.'

Father Paddy muttered his mumbo jumbo, sprinkled Holy Water on the coffin while my mother wept and I stood iron-jawed and stoically dry-eyed, my fists clenched, while the words lodged in my throat.

And you, my father, there on that sad height,
Curse, bless, me now with your fierce tears, I pray.

Abstinence Makes the Heart Grow Fonder

Picture a sixteen year old boy, very ugly, crew cut, rotten teeth (calcium deficiencies), overbite, gawky, zit faced, sitting in an upright hard wooden pew in church in suit and tie.

Me.

Picture a church built on swampland, in between brown rushes and yellow festering water that breeds billions of mosquitoes, harbours a thousand croaking frogs.

Green River Baptist Church.

And now picture the congregation: men in dark suits and ties with wide lapels, women in long crinkly large dresses with high collars and puffy sleeves, and skirts down to the ground so their sinful ankles are hidden. Outside for sports events or swimming parties, girls wear their father's extra-large t-shirts over their bathing suits so that no flesh shows.

Them.

Picture a community where no one has sex, no one mentions sex, and every new born is a virgin birth. Sex is evil. Sex is the original sin that cast Adam and Eve out of paradise.

Now picture the Pastor of this church, a young preacher straight out of Riverside Bible School, with riveting eyes, a shock of blonde hair over his face, goofy teeth, and an iron grip on his congregation.

Pastor Steve.

Finally picture his Sunday sermons, at around eleven am on a Sunday, with flies buzzing around, us with rumbling stomachs (we've been in church and Sunday School and choir practice since 8 a.m.), in sweltering silence.

He was the only one allowed to talk about sex, but in euphemism, in the negative. *Flee fornication! Resist the devil! Trim your virgin lamps in preparation for the arrival of your bridegroom Christ.*

Procreation occurs only within the sanctity of marriage. Dating is frowned upon, dancing is forbidden and rock music a damnable sin. Boys and girls do not mingle at social events, and married couples are not encouraged to hold hands or display any affection for each other in public. There must be a Bible between you if seated next to a person of the opposite sex.

Seriously.

It was easy for me to be a virgin at that church: not only was I separated from the opposite sex and given no means, opportunity, or motive, I was, as previously mentioned, also very, very ugly. I hated the moustache beginning to grow, the hair on my legs, the breaking voice, the way puberty had stretched me into a gangly alien being who did not recognise himself in the mirror. And worst of all, my genitals had mutated slowly into monstrous alien beings with a life of their own, insisting on shaming me and diverting my attention from the straight and narrow at every social event. Hormones and pheromones and testosterones pumped through me, torturing me, possessing me, compelling me to stare down girl's tops, up their skirts, to rehearse vile imaginary acts my Id wanted to perform with them.

However when it came to actual sex, I was safe from Satan's clutches. I was the last person who ever would get laid, the least attractive to the opposite sex in that church. I would, it seemed, remain pure with lamps trimmed until the second coming of Jesus my Saviour.

But then there was Terri.

Terri was fourteen. For some reason unbeknown to me, she sat next to me in church every Sunday. A large Schofield King James hard cover, red letter, gold edged

Bible sat between us of course, but she always wore these huge long skirts with great big folds in them, like a king-size doona, and we managed to touch each other without anyone noticing. At first it was just an accident, my hand pressing against hers on the bench, my foot against her shin under the skirt. And then, slowly, over weeks, it was fingers and wrists. And then it became a habit: every Sunday we squeezed hands, palpitated fingers, felt the texture of sweaty palms throughout the whole service.

Every service.

I never got above the elbows, and she never did more than tickle my palms and squeeze my fingers tight as if she were milking them.

So far so good. Nothing wrong with a little hanky-panky. But things got worse. The pastor warned us about slippery slopes, about the little lie that becomes the big lie, about small habits that become lifestyles, about roads that are easy to run down that become, well, slippery slopes that shoot you straight down to hell.

So I don't know how this happened, but by the fifth service of Lent or whatever it was, my fingers were spidering over her thighs, and by Easter, (an extra-long service) her hand had guided me all over her legs, her armpits, the outside of her bra, her belly button, the long fence of her panty elastic, and finally, at the Eucharist, into a marshland where birds exploded out of the reeds as I walked past, the water oily and still and yellow and stinking like the primeval soup that spawned the first life on earth, where I waded in the water barefoot, squeezed through the brown reeds and plants that looked as if they would eat me, my feet getting stuck in the mud, and the terrifying pressure as I tried to pull them out of the suction vacuum. Strange creatures swam towards me. Water spiders skated on the surface of the viscous water. Bubbles erupted from the bottom, and my stomach was in a queasy knot of repulsive disgust and excitement at the adventure of it all. I felt the shame of returning home all muddy and stinking to mother.

Her face when I dared look was bright purple. Her breath caught.

'You all right, dear,' whispered her mother, turning her head from the pew ahead. 'Do you need your asthma spray?'

Terri shook her head. 'I'm fine, Mum.'

The Pastor was always watching. Like God. He knew the number of hairs on our head. He was Omnipresent, Omniscient and Omnipotent. Wore yellow rimmed glasses when he read from the huge Bible on the huge pulpit and peered over them at anyone fidgeting or coughing or not paying attention.

But in a private universe flocks of birds beat hot wings at me, dive bombed me from dizzying heights, cawed loudly in my ears. The ground beneath my feet crumbled away and I found myself in quicksand that sucked and sucked and squeezed me down into a dark abyss.

Like Molasses. Like treacle. Like honey. Like. Like. Like.

This could not go on.

But next Sunday, it did go on. This time I had entered another dimension, a shimmering world of high crystal clear lakes and tall mountains, snow-capped, with clear blue skies. The blue lakes were transparent and through the still skin of viscous water I could see mermaids, alien creatures, coloured tropical fish.

Next Sunday, I who had never taken any drug or mind altering substance in my life was high, my brain blowing out beyond language into wordless ecstasy, seeing colours that were beyond the spectrum, hearing choirs singing outside of the human auditory range, feeling my body expand and pulse as large as the universe. And the portal was a viscous stickiness between my fingers that felt like snot but tasted like sour grapefruit.

A month of Sundays later, the same. A sticky dimension of pure spirit, a transubstantiation of the flesh.

Every Sunday. Every. Every. Every.

All under the watchful eye of the Pastor, who stared omnisciently, but, I prayed fervently, saw nothing.

I tried to stop, and one Sunday refused to unclasp my hands, sat on them, gripped the hymnal tight to my chest. But she wriggled and sighed and pushed against my thigh until I let my hand loll on the pew bench, and she groped for it and guided my fingers into her parallel universe. Every week. Sometimes we toured her belly button, traversing vast territories of desert, jungle, mountains, across rivers, slowly, finding the source of the Nile. Sometimes I was in her armpit, or following the contours of her bra, and while our faces were deadpan during a long sermon about sodomy (*Furthermore, since they did not think it worthwhile to retain the knowledge of God, he gave them over to a depraved mind, to do what ought not to be done*), we would be under the ramparts and into lands of cloud kingdoms made of candy floss, or discovering King Solomon's Mines full of glittering treasure, or running fast down a mountain pass during a thunderstorm, while lightning crackled all around us. I say us, but can only speak for myself. Her mouth remained prim and tight; her eyes never met mine; her posture was upright and her demeanour pious. The only give away was the facial rosacea, the sunburn spreading down her neck and on occasions the goose pimples on her arm.

And every session would end in the closing plangencies of the sermon, after which the congregation would leap to its feet, grab its hymnbooks and sing.

Stand up stand up for Jesus, ye soldiers of the cross.
Ye must not suffer loss.

Every Sunday night I would rebuke myself for these carnal ventures into sin, and vow never to give in to lust again, but the following week, Terri and I made our ways into caves, through waterfalls, across purple fields of little flowers into new worlds where three suns rose, and seven moons orbited, and citizens wore bright and shiny auras around their middles.

It had to stop.

We climbed hot dunes, above a crashing glitter blue sea; we dived the Great Barrier Reef and marvelled at a million species of coral; we danced on a wild tropical Hawaiian beach in hula skirts, drinking Kava from half coconut shells; we orbited the earth in silver UFOs with friendly green aliens with a thousand tube fingers like mini elephant trunks that sucked at our skin instead of speaking though their mouths.

And the sermons continued, like thunder rolling across the sky. A storm was coming, that was for sure. Fist on pulpit, eagle eyes, tremulous voice: *Do not be deceived: neither the sexually immoral, nor idolaters, nor adulterers, nor men who practise homosexuality, nor thieves, nor the greedy, nor drunkards, nor revilers, nor swindlers will inherit the kingdom of God.*

Birds exploded out of the reeds, cawing loudly in fright. Cicadas screeched. A billion frogs croaked, and mosquitoes zinged around my flesh, biting me where I dared not scratch.

'That tickles.' Terri wriggled in her seat.

Soft breezes blew over the sun scorched dunes, and the briny sea, hot, tangled with seaweed, the tide pulsing in and out, slopped inside of me. The castaway clawed his way to the top of the dune to discover that this indeed was an island, and he was surrounded on all sides by glittering blue sea as far as the eye could see.

And then she giggled. The sermon screeched to a halt. Terri hid her face in her hair. I frowned into my Bible.

'If people find the Word of the Lord amusing,' Pastor Steve said to the rafters above us, 'then they should crawl out of this sacred place on their bellies, like a serpent.'

The silence was a high snowy mountain in a rushing wind. My fingers were frost bitten. My lips chapped with cold. The high pitched whine rose in my left ear, and my feet were icy. Fishes nibbled on my fingertips.

His blue, blue eyes watching, watching, through his yellow rimmed spectacles. 'OK at the back there? Let's continue.'

But thank the Lord: the organ finally struck up the rousing post-sermon hymn and the congregation rose to its feet. Terri smoothed her dress. I held the hymnal open at the wrong place, the thin pages sticking to my fingers as I turned them.

Stand up, stand up for Jesus, stand in His strength alone;
The arm of flesh will fail you, ye dare not trust your own.

After the service, Terri was hustled out by her parents, but before I could escape, Pastor Steve blocked my way. 'Jimmy, I'd like to see you at the manse this afternoon. Are you free?'

Freight trains screeched in my ears.

It was nothing. It was a routine visit, I told myself. We all took turns at visiting the pastor for spiritual check-ups. Nothing. Nothing. Nothing.

The manse, a large double storey house, stood high on the ridge behind the church.

'Come in, come in.' The Pastor's office streamed natural light, and he sat behind an immense oak desk, surrounded by bookshelves filled with books like *The Corinthian Catastrophe*, *Fox's Book of Martyrs* etc. He gave me a bone-breaking handshake. Toothy smile. 'Tell me about Terri,' he said.

'Who?'

He closed his eyes and then opened them, as if he had sent a quick Instagram prayer to God and received an answer. 'This has got to stop.'

I reddened.

'Satan,' says the Pastor, 'is a roaring lion seeking whom he may devour. And he is a good counterfeiter. He deceives young people into thinking that lust is love, that mere feelings are the real thing. And many a young person has perished in this way.'

He slid a gold edged bible onto the table towards me. 'I Corinthians chapter 6, verse 18. Read the passage I chose for you today. Aloud, please.'

I cleared my throat. 'Flee fornication,' I read.

'Go on.'

'Every sin that a man doeth is without the body; but he that committeth fornication sinneth against his own body.'

The pastor had X-ray vision. His eyes could melt anything in their path. I was a puddle of red shame on the floor.

'I'm not trying to condemn you, Jimmy. My job is to protect my lost sheep from prowling wolves.'

I opened my mouth, but no words came out.

'Fornication is a sin against your own body. You understand that? Your body is the temple of the Holy Spirit.'

I pictured a temple, somewhere in India – dark, winding passages, of high spiralling towers into the tropical sky.

Hundreds of birds wheeling around its turrets. Cawing loudly like crows.

'Sorry.'

He stood behind me. 'Don't apologise to me. Apologise to Him whose temple you have defiled.' He guided me with a hand to the rough floorboards in front of his desk where we kneeled, and he pressed fingers into my skull until it hurt. 'Begone Satan! Lord, give Jimmy armour to combat the weakness of the flesh, weapons to fight the son of darkness.'

'Amen.'

I blinked up at him.

'Imagine a big black marker. A huge black marker, the size of a person, dripping black ink. Paint her from head to toe with it. Blot her out. The lustful images you have saved in your heart of her – black them out. Scribble over her. Cover her with ink.'

I imagined. The marker squeaked as I pressed hard.

'Jimmy, if your eye causes you to lust, gouge it out and throw it away. It is better for you to lose one part of your body than for your whole body to be thrown into hell. Do you understand that?'

I nodded.

He stood. Mussed my hair. 'God bless you, Jimmy. Black her out of your life. Zip her in a shroud. Delete her from your hard drive. Sacrifice her to God. Then He will give you the desires of your heart.'

'Thank you Pastor Steve.'

Next Sunday I sat as far away from Terri as I could. I could not look her in the eye. Not that I had ever looked her in the eye. Not once.

She glared past me, in bewilderment, in hurt, in scorn. And as she left the service afterwards, her body brushed against me. 'Coward!'

That night I dreamed of dead bodies floating on the Ganges River, floating past temples spattered with bird excrement. Of Easter Island statues, abandoned, toppled in the grass, while the glitter blue sea crashed on the shores of this lonely island. Forlorn birds cawed in alarm, wheeling overhead in large circles.

She was hurt, but I could not do this anymore. I scribbled her with the marker, blotted her from my retina. She sat with her parents in negative afterimage.

At school we learned that the Mississippi delta was an anti-climax of a river that silted up at the end, went underground, flooded all marshy and sticky with reeds growing in the estuary, with lots of creatures swimming in its yellow slime.

And so it went. I had resisted the devil and he had fled from me. I felt pretty sanctimonious, holy even, and Pastor Steve smiled at me from the pulpit.

But on the third Sunday after Lent, she passed me a note during the meet-and-greet-your-brethren part of the service.

Kitchen. After service. Parents have to talk to Pastor S. We have ten minutes max.

I should ignore it. Be alert and of sober mind. Your enemy the devil prowls around like a roaring lion looking for someone to devour. I tore the note into shreds throughout the service, each word, until it was million pieces of dandruff.

But after the service, Terri was waiting for me. She pushed me to the back of the church kitchen, amongst the boxes and the cupboard and closets.

'Hi, Terri.'

'Hi.'

'Sorry,' I said.

'Sure you are.'

'We're leaving the country tomorrow,' she said.

121

'Leaving?'

'You'll never see me again from tomorrow. Are you happy about that?' She pressed herself against me, and guided my hand under her skirt.

We fumbled in the pantry amidst stale chocolate chip cookies and cakes under doilies and large urns of water heating up for tea. We didn't take off any clothes.

A black night sky enveloped me and pin prick coloured stars fizzed at my brain. I smelled burnt rice and gas.

There was not much to see, and for me not much to feel except terror, pain and dizzy weightlessness that made my whole body spin into the far reaches of space. Terri winced, clawed, and breathed much too loud, as if she were suffering a stroke, but we both got through it.

'Jesus,' she said. 'Christ.'

And then we smoothed down clothes, pulled up pants, straightened hair. We didn't even talk to each other. We walked out the back door onto the lawn where trestle tables were waiting for us. Terri's parents whisked her away by car, and I was left with a thumping heart. I looked up and saw, through a pane of glass into the office, the eyes of Pastor Steve, watching, watching, watching.

Terrorist

A 'qualified gook', the Sergeant Major called him. The man knew all the enemy's plans against us, the location of guerrilla base camps and arms caches, the location and layout of the enemy command centres. Normally, such evil vermin (again the Sergeant Major's words) were zapped, slotted, scribbled, eliminated, wasted on the spot. Futile, he said, to take such scum prisoner, bring them to court only to sentence them to death. The State of Emergency gave soldiers in the field the powers to execute justice. But this case was different. This terrorist must be kept alive – orders from high up – so that we could extract information from him.

'He's a big fish, and I want you to look after this terrorist this weekend, Wilson.'

'A terrorist, sir?'

'He's the commissar of a large group, and he's been swimming in a hell of a lot of shit. The treatment card will be given to you by the doctor as soon as he's had a look at the patient. You take it from there. He's all yours.'

'Sir.'

Medics, army patients and staff watched at the hospital entrance as the Sergeant Major wheeled the terrorist in on a stretcher. One medic walked by his side, holding up a drip which obscured my view of his face. As they wheeled him into theatre, a limping man in pyjamas bumped the stretcher. 'Kill the fucken gook.'

I waited outside the theatre for the doctor to give me instructions. Two men brushed past me with notebooks but the Sergeant Major barred their way. 'Sorry, gentlemen, you won't be able to begin work on him for a few days. He's being heavily sedated with morphine and needs intensive care for the next twenty-four hours. Once he's in the ward you can return.'

The short-cropped blond man held up a manicured hand in protest. 'Our instructions are not to leave the patient for one minute. He must be handcuffed to the bed at all times.'

'Gentlemen, he won't even be able to open his eyes for a day or two. Nevertheless, we'll give you beds in the ward.'

'It must be a private ward,' butted in the other soft-spoken man. I noted his polished brown crocodile-hide shoes, his closely clipped fingernails. He smelled of soap.

'Suit yourself,' said the Sergeant Major, arms up in mock surrender. 'I'm just in charge of this hospital.'

'We wouldn't like to risk anything happening to the patient,' said the blond man. 'He must speak to no one but us, and no one must have contact with him, except the medic treating him. We'll bring in his food, take him to the toilet.'

The Sergeant Major pointed to me – I hovered in the corridor. 'Corporal Wilson is the man assigned to treat your patient. He's our brightest new medic here. And very good at such menial tasks.'

Six blue eyes focused on me for a moment. A curt nod from one man, a sweep from head to toe from the other, and a hooded frown from the Sergeant Major. I stood to attention and saluted.

'All yours, Corporal,' said the doctor as he handed over the RX1033 treatment form.

'Ward six,' said the Sergeant Major. The theatre door opened and the stretcher poked its way out; a naked foot banged against the door. I could see the face: eyes shut, wild hair, cracked lips, dry skin, stubbly chin. The two security men jumped into action, marching behind me as I wheeled my charge through the throng of patients. The drip swung from the stand attached to the head of the stretcher, and a tube disappeared under the sheet. My eyes had already located a widening brown stain, at shin level.

Once I had transferred my new patient from the stretcher, I followed the doctor's instructions. Treatment was to begin immediately and was simple: apply Glisterine and Ichthamnol dressing, bathe and clean wounds with Cetramol every day, watch for gangrene and sepsis, administer antibiotic injections QID, give drip for first three days only, decreasing the quantity gradually.

Glisterine and Ichthamnol (Glick 'n Ick as we called it) was a gleaming brown/black sticky substance like molasses with healing properties and when applied to wounds, halted septicaemia, encouraged new growth and bound fibres.

To my consternation, when I walked back into the ward with the large jar of Glick 'n Ick in my hands, my patient lay awake, his milky eyes assessing me. The two men paced the room, waiting for him to recover his wits sufficiently so they could begin their interrogations. The first act they had performed while I was out was to hand-cuff a limp hand to the bedpost. I checked the drip, strapped and bound to his other arm and suspended on a metal stand. A steady saline solution flowed into his vein.

I pulled the sheet aside. He wore boxer shorts and a T-shirt. I noticed at first only surface wounds, pieces of flesh gouged out here and there, but no internal damage. I judged he had been hit by shrapnel from some sort of mine. I noted two gunshot wounds where bullets had grazed the skin and tumbled into fleshy areas of the thigh and shoulder. Then, when I lifted the sheet covering his legs, I started: the left leg was a stump cut off below the knee. Why hadn't this been indicated on the treatment form? I unwound soiled bandages that stuck to bits of flesh, until I exposed a weeping pink ball. I looked up to see if this hurt, but he showed a stoic front, oblivious to the squeamish tingling in my gut.

125

The leg wasn't gangrenous, but pus-white plasma had grown over the inflamed areas. I scratched the pus off with an abrasive pad and then swabbed it with cotton wool dipped in Cetramol. The leg flinched.

'Did that hurt?'

The terrorist looked at the two men and I saw the hint of an ironic smile on his face. He shook his head. The two men peered at the wound. 'Oh, my God,' said one. 'I can't take this.' The other tapped his shoulder. 'Doc, we'll be outside in the tearoom. Don't leave until we get back.'

'It doesn't look that bad,' I said to the terrorist. For a second, his eyes swirled into life, then the milky blankness covered them again, and I returned to work. The operation took quite a while. Each wound oozed yellow fluid. I cleaned until the flesh gleamed pink and shiny. I covered everything with Glick 'n Ick, then wrapped the wounds in clean crepe bandages, which immediately soiled with the brown ointment.

When the security officers returned, the terrorist, who had been staring at my medic badge, closed his eyes.

'Thanks, Doc,' said the blond man.

The treatment continued for weeks. Every day I found the two interrogators in the room, one taking notes, the other pacing the room in his crocodile shoes, asking questions and waiting for the patient to reply. I only caught snatches of the conversations, for as soon as I came in, the blond man would slap his book shut and say, 'That's enough for now. Let's take a break.' And they would leave me to unravel bandages, swab pus, dab black plasma on plastic pink flesh, give antibiotic injections, check for bedsores.

The terrorist watched every move I made, every nervous tic in my manner, every shifty glance I stole at him. He showed interest in all the proceedings, obliging and assisting me in any way he could, rolling over at appropriate moments, or raising his leg, or nodding for me to go on when I thought it hurt too much. When the Security Branch men came into the room, he looked dull, opaque, sullen, stupid. But as soon as they were gone, he radiated intelligence.

Medical training had taught me to see the patient as a machine to be jabbed, stitched up, patched. To see him in any other way could be disastrous. How could you suture, cut open or inject if you knew you were doing this to a human being, or if you could imagine how it felt? But here lay my first patient insisting on being human. Instead of an inert object to work on, I had a being who watched me, who breathed, and exhibited a tunnel of thoughts that brightened and faded, like mine. And what was worse, this man was no ordinary patient but an Enemy of the State.

'I'm sorry.'

'No, it doesn't hurt.'

This was the first time he spoke to me. Here was a real live terrorist, a man who had been trained to kill, had swum across bordering rivers with Claymore anti-personnel mines strapped to his back, who had lived on turtles, and had probably murdered, raped and (of course) terrorised people.

'How is the leg?' he asked.

'The sepsis should be gone in a few days.'

'You're a good doctor.'

'I'm not a doctor.' The body, I meant to say, is a miraculous instrument with mechanisms to heal itself. Blood congeals, lymphatic fluid seals the wounds, allowing new fibres to grow, then a scab protects the delicate process of regrowth, until it is as good as new. Well... I looked at the stump of his leg... almost.

'You look too young to be in the army. Too young to be so good at medicine.'

'I'm serving my country.'

A medical officer walked into the room to get some Betadine. I adopted – reflexively – a brusque attitude in bandaging the patient, pulling the bandage tight, treating him as an inert object. But when the officer left, the terrorist smiled. 'What is your name?'

'Steven. Steve.' I dabbed a wound with Cetramol, checking the yellowed gauze for sepsis.

'I'm J.J,' he said. 'Comrade J. J.'

Another week went by. I had checked on my patient's progress daily, and every time I entered the room he looked relieved to abandon the wooden expression he had to create for the questioning officers. I was surprised at how much information he contained. They spent hours each day coaxing it out of him. All day, every day he talked, his lips drying, his face expressionless, and all those facts, figures, names, places, code numbers poured into their notebooks. Soon the Air Force would be bombing training camps, arms caches would be located, villages would be visited, terrorist sympathisers arrested.

But something else began growing in me too: guilt at my secret conspiracy with the enemy. I switched to slit-eyed efficiency when they looked up at me in surprise, following the patient's smile. I was in league with the man, even though I had said or done nothing to indicate any disloyalty to my uniform. Whatever it was, guilt oozed through me whenever they saw me interacting with him, dressing his wounds. They whispered to each other, pointing at his obliging movement of an arm or the considerate way this medic dabbed his wounds.

'You have a scar in your heart.'

The interrogators were out of the room. 'Sorry?'

128

'I can see. You are troubled,' he said. 'Is it woman trouble?'

'There's no trouble.'

'It's woman trouble.'

The words were out before I knew what they were. 'I don't know. She's... I don't know.'

'You've given her all the power.' He smiled so broadly that I could see all his teeth and his pink gums.

'No.'

His laugh sounded like an old lorry starting up. 'It's true. And that's when relationships go bad. That means trouble.'

'I don't understand her. I don't know where I stand with her. I don't understand...'

'You expect to understand her?' Here he started up his engine again. 'One day, my friend, I must give you some advice about relationships.'

After all these weeks of dressings, interrogations and dabbings, I began to look forward to my daily routine and expurgation. Day by day, I proved my worth as a medic. My apprenticeship in the hospital demonstrated competence and the Sergeant Major seemed happy with the way I had handled my first case. Soon, he promised, I would be ready to be sent out to the frontline. And the conversation and meeting of eyes with the patient comforted me too, I argued to myself. It meant I was good at my job; I was bringing him back to life, healing this man and making him more and more human. Our conversations grew easier, more fluid. I told him more and more about Bianca; he gave me advice. It became a habit I looked forward to.

But one day I walked into the ward and found an empty bed: no terrorist, no interrogators, no healing fibres.

129

He's escaped. Or they've moved him to another ward, now that he's healing. Or they've discovered I was being too familiar with the enemy and have discreetly moved him away. I knocked on the Sergeant Major's door.

'Wilson, what can I do for you?'

'Sir, I… the prisoner, the terrorist?'

'Oh,' he smiled. 'We should have told you…'

'Have you moved him?'

'Wilson, you did a very good job on those wounds. I must say, I'm very pleased with your treatment. I'm going to recommend that you qualify as a fully-fledged medic.'

I nodded my head. 'You mean he's been discharged?'

He laughed. 'Discharged. Yes, you might say that, Wilson. You did a fine job. That weekend pass you wanted? Take it. Enjoy your weekend.' He pulled up some papers in front of his face. 'Dismissed.'

'Sir.' I saluted, stiffly backing out. 'Thank you, sir.'

Much later I discovered the truth. The two interrogators had found out all they needed to know from him, had closed their notebooks, and squeaked out of the hospital in their crocodile shoes. The terrorist was put in a prison truck and driven to the capital where he was tried in camera, sentenced to death for crimes of terrorism, and hanged a few days later.

Application for Position as Failure

Dear Sir/ Madam

I wish to apply for the position you advertised in the Daily Sun. Although my expertise is in self-obliteration and self-worth (or lack of), and my work mainly in disappointment, I do have much experience in failure, which this letter will strive to illustrate.

Please find below a brief summary of my work experience.

I have been a failure since I was four years old. From the very start, I was ambitious, and set my hopes high. I wanted too much out of life and consequently came short. I wanted to be somebody and became nobody.

My early career aspirations were lofty: writer, film maker, movie star, musician. I have been a consistent failure at each: my first love was film. All through my childhood, I played out Cowboy and Indian battles in my head; I sketched out intricate plots of murder mysteries where the murderer hid behind shadows of shadows of other characters, I ran and reran in my head (complete with sound track) wild adventures in darkest Africa; I acted out scenes of survivors clawing up endless sand dunes to reach imaginary oases. I was brimming with ideas. I spent weeks and months and years making plasticine frame-by-frame animations of little space creatures on Mars. I sent off proposals to Hollywood, grant proposals to Disney, samples to Tisch School of the Arts in New York. I aspired; I dreamed. I was destined to be the next Lukas, Spielberg, Goddard.

It had to happen, I thought, because I believed it so strongly.

It didn't.

A strong component of failure is the willingness to try again and again. It is the belief in success that gives me the edge in this regard.

At twelve, I learned to play the guitar, keyboard, drums. I was going to be the next Hendrix, Santana, Bon Jovi. Behind closed bedroom doors, I mimed my way through teenage-hood to Nirvana, eyes closed, headphones clamped to my head, in front of imaginary crowds cheering, and screaming women wetting their pants. I made it into a school band, but at the first and last Battle of the Bands competition I played in, we came dead last.

Most of all, I wanted to be a best-selling author, a paperback writer, a Nobel Prize winner. I spent my university days writing out plot summaries, listing titles of books I would write, discussing Literature with other would-be writers in clouds of cigarette smoke. All through my twenties, I wrote novels, none of which are complete, and none of which have been published. I submitted them to over two hundred publishers. I wrote for every competition imaginable; I sliced off pieces of my soul at each attempt. Each rejection was a blow to an already over-bruised soul.

I was close once. Black Bird Publishers wanted to see my novel called Fail! (about a failed writer), and suggested I rewrite it. I rewrote it. Can you change the title, and the main character? Make him more... positive? Sure. And the ending more upbeat? Of course. Less of a loser? Sure, sure. Ultimately, however, they had to reject it, calling it a critical failure (I enclose the letter for your perusal in lieu of a letter of recommendation, which they would not give me).

I enclose no other letters of recommendation. Unfortunately, all those I approached did not get back to me, or those who did, couldn't remember who I was, or what I had achieved.

My experience is deep and broad and painful. For those who say 'Failure is not an option' and then fail, the caverns they carve in their own flesh are huge. Let no one say I have lived a shallow life. My wounds go deep.

As for my personal life – my relationships have been consistently dysfunctional. I fell in love many times, and never once has love been reciprocated, except on rare occasions when my partner sought to exploit me for whatever reason, or to use me for some self-aggrandizing project of his or her own. My first love was a girl called Denise (13), but being too tongue-tied and inept at fourteen, I watched her affection grow cold and finally shrink to nothing as she walked off with my best friend into a private sunset of their own. My nearest approximation of success – I could smell it – occurred when I met a model whom I courted and wooed online. She invited me to L.A. I flew on intercontinental Virgin wings, arrived with expensive bottles of wine and nervous plans of seduction and lifelong romance, but at that first meeting – she could smell failure – she informed me that a new boyfriend had somehow materialised, and that I could stay as long as I wanted as long as I didn't come anywhere near her.

Academically, I have taken the less travelled road. I spent three years studying a B.A. (a 'bugger all' as my father called this arts degree), and could not find a job after I finished so I stayed and did Honours. Again, I was unemployed. I applied for a Master of Arts and spent two years doing that. No, it was not a success. I failed well. I laboured through academic jargon, literary theory, wrote a tortuous and tortured dissertation on an obscure topic, lodged the thesis in a library, and no one read it. But I rose to the ranks of graduate assistant, exploited part time tutor, and in lieu of a PhD, I took on the mantle of failed academic. I was always snubbed by sharper critics, and felt dull and slow in their presence.

Applying for jobs brought me a sea of rejection slips to rival my writing failures. Finally I was begrudgingly given a temporary position at a second rate business firm (ranked 2421 out of 2423 in Forbes Magazine) because the person they wanted to hire was unavailable and I was a temporary stand in. I was a ghost, never seen, never given an office – no one remembered my name or what I was doing there. In time the permanent position became available: I applied for it, and it was given to a young graduate with large front teeth (not that I have anything against large front teeth).

My patron saint is St Jude.

Failure, of course, is only measurable by aspiration: I wanted to be a brilliant mind, a creative, famous writing personality, someone whom everyone would whisper after and say 'there he is!' – a musician of exceptional talent who pioneered a new wave of sound. I could have performed artistic miracles. But… But… I have instead a resume filled with regret.

My soul has taken a battering, and if it were visible, you would see the scars, the marks of history. Like a sponge, it absorbs the poison of society, and now is officially disabled. The shape of failure shadows me everywhere: I have a perpetual psychological limp.

Would you be interested in such a person? I am large enough to continue without hope, and idealistic enough to march into more pain.

I have the energy, the drive, the blackness in me to fulfil this position.

I look forward to hearing from you, although I know I won't.

Thank you for your consideration.

Yours truly,

Uncle

Uncle moves slowly, eats far too much. His eyes are yellow. He watches her sideways when facing the TV.

'How long is uncle staying?'

Her mother lowers her voice. 'Be nice to him. Without him we would be in trouble. We owe him a lot.'

'But he will leave soon, won't he?'

'Well,' says her mother, 'he's here to help us get on our feet again. As soon as we're on our feet, he will feel OK about us being on our own. It's not good for a family to be on their own.'

'We're not on our own. There's you and me.'

'I mean without a father, a man of the house.'

The first time she is so thrown she cannot even know what happened. She crawls to the bathroom and washes away the blood. She is nine years old.

The second time he takes her to the shed behind the mosque. It smells of fuel and the sewerage from the nearby grey water system. Cardboard darkens the window; spades and running shears and rakes cover the walls; the workbench gives her splinters. He pulls his dirty white thawb over him. 'You're a good girl, Amina.'

The third time it happens on her tenth birthday. She suffers herself to be dressed up and served up as a delicious feast to her relatives who coo and fuss and gush. Such a pretty young girl. See this photo? The family huddles together (cheese! cheese!) her brother acts the clown, prodding the air with two antenna fingers of peace, she smiles harder than the rest, and her tears are air brushed away. She holds her fists tightly over her stomach.

'Where have you been Amina?'

'We went for a little walk around the compound,' says her uncle.

She wears a red and white dress, a red bow in her black shining hair which cascades down her shoulders like two waterfalls. Her white bobby socks have been pulled tight over her ankles; and no one notices that her white shoes are scuffed with sawdust. She wears blood red lipstick. Her left leg is slightly bent and arched. Her smile is sweet, but her black eyes burn. Her uncle stands behind her, his hands on her shoulders and she does not flinch. Her mother watches from the side. A happy family.

After photos, her mother presents her with a cake, ten candles in a circle on the green icing. 'What did you do to your hair, Amina? It's full of sawdust. And don't suck your thumb!'

The baker has imposed a ghostly photo of her on the cake. A five year old icing princess smiles at her. She makes her wish, blows out the candles, and cuts the slices. She has to hold the knife with two hands to stop trembling. She slices the picture of herself into seven pieces, cutting through her eyes, lips, nose and forehead.

Your wish, Amina?

A birthday wish is a secret. She clenches it in her fist behind her back. She can't eat any cake. She has to bite her lip so she will not throw up.

'Delicious. Have some, Amina, my little princess!' He lifts her chin.

She unwraps her presents, reacts to each. *Sucran.* Thanks everyone. Thank you. The biggest present of all stands in the corner, the climax of the party. Everyone knows what is coming. Amina will love this, she has wanted this for so long!

A bicycle, a beautiful Barbie pink bicycle with tassels on the handlebars.

'Say something, Amina! Aren't you going to say thank you to your uncle for such a wonderful present?'

A shadow falls between her body and her heart.

'Did you hear me? Where are you, Amina? Amina the dreamer!'

She smiles. 'Thank you, uncle.'

She paints the Barbie bike blue, tears off the tassels and turns it into a BMX that can plough through the mud, ramp over concrete rubble. She peels off the smiling Barbie glitter stickers and replaces them with NO FEAR and BLISS QUEEN.

She brings him his food, his Pepsi in a can, opened and fizzing. He thumbs his prayer beads and watches her. Always. Even when she goes to the toilet. She showers lightning fast when he is out of the house, and at night props her desk against the bedroom door, which does not lock.

The fourth time. The fifth time. The tenth time. She loses count. 'Good girl,' he says; and, 'If you tell anyone, I will kill you.'

She prays that God will do something. If not, she will have to take matters in her own hands. She fantasises about Doing the Deed. Maybe next time he visits her room, she will hide two knives up her sleeves and will plunge them into his eyes. Or if she has a gun, she will shoot and shoot and shoot and he will twitch and fall and crumple. Or in the shed she will pull the whole workbench of tools on top of him, and when he opens his mouth to cry for help, she will pour petrol down his throat and set him alight. Flames will roar out of his mouth. Next time... Next time... The fantasies roll around in her mind like marbles, so loud she is afraid others might hear.

He drives a fat car with an engine that roars like a wounded camel. His car is his baby, he says, and he loves it more than he loves life itself. He spends hours polishing it, revving the engine with the hood up. He tints the windows, tinkers with tappets and spark plugs, paints stripes down the side.

If she wants to hurt him, she will have to hurt his car.

Today he has gone off with friends in a Land Cruiser for some dune surfing. He will be out all day. Her friend Nouf and Amina stand in the garage. The car grimaces at them.

'An ugly beast,' says Nouf.

Amina picks up a rusty nail, unscrews the cap of the back tyre hub and presses the little pin inside the valve so that the air hisses out.

'What are you doing, Amina?'

'I saw someone do this.'

The tyre flattens. 'Escape, little friends,' says Amina. 'You're free now. Fly! Fly!'

'You're crazy Amina, who are you talking to, the air? The air is not a person.'

'Let's do the other tyres.'

'Let's get out of here.'

The car squats heavily on its rims.

The next morning her uncle leaves the house for work. He always cuts it fine, leaving at the last moment, and screaming off at full throttle. But today he unlocks the driver side door and stops. Stares. Circles the car. He peers up at the apartment complex. Amina and Nouf pull back. He bangs his fist on the bonnet. Checks each tyre again. He checks his watch, pounds off into the hot sun towards Al Corniche roundabout to hail a taxi.

Nouf giggles into her sleeve. Amina's heart beats so fast it hurts. But she feels good.

They watch in the 40 degree heat. They listen to his footsteps crunch over stones and shell rubble to the Corniche roundabout where he waits in the dust devils of a Gulf summer morning. Even as he stoops to get in the back seat of the taxi, he stares up at the amber apartment complex, scanning, as if he means to catch a glimpse of the guilty person.

'He can't see us from here.' They shrink into the shadows but when the taxi speeds off into the brown smudge of the city, Amina and Nouf dance on the balcony, waving their hands and pulling faces. Amina pirouettes in a dance of victory. She knows she will become addicted to this feeling.

In the evening her uncle arrives back from work.

'Amina? Nouf?'

He blocks their way. The sweat has necklaced around his thawb, and the low sky has plastered his hair onto his head. Amina clutches Nouf's hand. Her heart is pulsing like a toad. 'No, Uncle, we didn't...'

'Did you see anyone in the garage this morning, Or last night?'

Nouf pulls back her hair, wide-eyed. 'No, Mr Darwish, we didn't see anything. Is there something wrong?'

'I'm going to find Mahmoud! It was those boys, I swear it.'

Amina and Nouf scurry off, holding their mouths. Mahmoud is a neighbourhood boy their age, and his gang frequents the car park to play games, or to throw stones at stray cats.

They watch from the balcony. Mahmoud and the boys

shake their heads in vehement innocence. Amina hears the echo of her uncle's backhand slap.

A child should not have to worry about her family's financial situation. But Amina takes on the stress of her mother's bills and bank account woes. 'Your father has sent us no money this month,' says her mother. Or: there is no money for bread today. Sorry.

Except for their benefactor. Uncle. He pays the bills. In return, he is master of the house.

She cannot lock her bedroom door or the bathroom door, and wherever she turns, the kind family uncle beckons, concerned about her welfare, taking her out in his car to the park so she can play. 'If you tell anyone,' he says, 'you will die.'

'You will die,' she tells herself. 'One day I will make it happen. One day.'

She dreams of a knight who will arrive one day and rescue her, who will banish the evil uncle to hell. Kill him. Disembowel him with a scimitar so that his wriggling intestines snake all over the sand and his frog heart quivers in the dust and his jelly brain is spilled over the tarmac. His body will be cut up into little pieces, his eyes skewered on the tip of the sword. The knight takes off his helmet, and she looks up at him. In fright she sees the knight is a woman with long black hair, black eyes and chocolate skin who answers to the name of Amina.

The fantasies grow into steel resolve. The glass plate thickens around her heart. She feels nothing now but rage.

'I want to kill my uncle.'

Nouf laughs. 'Why?'

'Will you help me?'

It is a game to Nouf. 'How will we do it?'

'His car. We cut the brakes so he hurtles off a cliff.'

'There are no cliffs. How about we poison him with cyanide?'

'Where would we get it?'

'We shoot him with a gun. Ha. Ha. Bang.'

'We fill his pillow with razor blades so he cuts himself to death when he sleeps.'

'Amina?' She cautions her friend who is pushing open her uncle's bedroom door.

'It's OK, he's out for the whole day. And we'll hear his car when he returns...'

'Your mother?'

'Out too.'

She pushes into his room; gags at the smell.

'Maybe we can set his room alight when he's asleep.'

Nouf rummages through the chest of drawers. 'Look what I found.'

'I don't think we should look in his clothes...'

'His wallet. With bank cards. Loads of them.'

'No cash?'

'No cash, but look at this...'

She holds a bank card in her two fingers. 'We can't get money unless we know the password.'

'Amina, you're evil.'

'How do you crack a password?'

'Usually it's something like your birthday or your favourite food, or a loved one.'

'Aha.'

'Nouf, what is it?'

'Look. Look! A DVD.'

'*Teen Bitches*? Why would he have this in his clothes?'

'I don't want to look at this.'

'Let's play it.' Nouf blows the dust off the TV/DVD player on the desk.

'No, Nouf.'

Nouf clicks on the remote. 'Make sure no one comes in.'

The images sear themselves onto her mind. But Nouf finds it funny. 'Is that what men do to women?'

'No,' says Amina. 'No.' She pulls at the DVD but it does not eject. Presses all the buttons to stop it, but it jams. 'We've broken it.'

'Let me try.'

Nouf digs in the machine with a pen. The DVD half ejects and she snaps off a piece.

'What do we do now?' A dark abyss opens beneath her feet.

Nouf yanks hard and the DVD splinters into slivers of light. She fishes out the pieces. 'Great.'

'Now what do we do?' Amina imagines sticking the pieces together with glue but she knows it will not work. You can't repair DVDs. She knows that.

Nouf stuffs the pieces back into the sleeve. 'Sorry, Teen Bitches,' she says. 'Too bad.'

They slide the DVD back under the bed covers, smooth over the clothes and retreat. But a black hole widens in Amina's heart.

'What is it?'

'Maybe we should just...'

Nouf nods. 'Better than...'

It is Amina who stuffs the DVD into a plastic bag, wraps it around itself and plunges it deep into the garbage bin, thrusting her arm in all the stinking food waste to bury it at the bottom of the week's offal.

'Feel better?'

Amina nods.

'Now let's make a vow. Swear never to do that.'

'Do what?'

'What those teen bitches were doing on the video.'

She is about to say something to Nouf, but thinks better of it. What words would she use? And if she uses no words, then it never happened. Never happens. Never will happen again.

Poverty is not a virtue. It makes you inferior. You are morally at fault somehow; you have done something bad. And at family gatherings she feels shame for her mother, for the condescension, the pity, the charity shown by the neighbours and the extended family. Everyone else has a husband. Everyone else has money. Her mother sits alone, unable to break into the bubble of wives knitted together by their banter about what latest handbags they have bought at the Centre, what the shops are like in the new Mall, their affectionate chastisement of their men.

'Why are you crying, Mama?'

'Your uncle is a good man. We have to appreciate what he does for us.

On Google, she checks how to cut brake cables, how to make a car veer and crash. She checks the shed. On the wall, a saw, a hammer, and on the table a vice. A hammer. She could simply reach for the hammer and beat his brain to a pulp. Or take two of those screwdrivers from that cabinet and plunge them into his eyes as he bows over her. With a little re-arranging…

She manoeuvres herself into position. In the dark she has rehearsed this. His feet find the tacks, his hands the razor blades, and his head the hammer and saw suspended at eye level. The acid bowl is balanced above the door.

She knows he has knocked the acid on himself by the screams. By the cursing. He rushes out into the heat, blood oozing from his hands, his hands on his face. 'Water! Water!'

Inside her head, she can see it happening. Will make it happen. But in the heat of the stinking day, it does not happen. Outside her head, life continues as it is fated to do, a relentless bulldozer of existence, crushing and flattening her into nothing. Nothing. Nothing.

It goes on. And on. And on. How many times, how many months, years? At thirteen, she makes up her mind. If he visits her again in her room, this will be the last time, she will scream as loud as she can, her mother will come running, God will hear, everyone will hear.

'I'll scream,' she tells him.

He pushes her head into a pillow and presses her face into the bed.

It is always from behind.

Why? she says. Why there?

He respects her virginity, he tells her, that's why.

Up until now it has been easier to disappear far behind her own walls into her own brain, and be a dead fish, a stone, something that cannot be hurt.

But now she has a new plan. He pushes her into the bathroom and locks them both in. As usual. But this time, while she is undressing and he is fumbling with his belt, she takes the key out of the door and flushes it down the toilet.

'Where's the key?'

'I don't know.'

He searches her clothes, his clothes, the shelves, the floor. Looks to see if it has been kicked under the door. She watches his fear now. They cannot be found together

145

in the toilet, she knows that. He stares at the window behind the toilet, which he will never fit through. 'Get dressed. Go out there. There must be another key, a spare key. Find it! Or get the Sudanese. Quick. Before your mother comes home.'

She is a snake of a girl, so she squeezes through, lands on the balcony and into the living room, goes straight out into the compound to find Nouf. They play until sunset, and when she returns two hours later, she finds her mother worried. 'Where have you been? Your uncle has locked himself in the bathroom, and can't find the key. He said he called you and called you and you didn't answer him.'

'I didn't hear him. I was out playing with Nouf.'

'Better call the Sudanese.'

The Sudanese man has to break the lock to get in. Her uncle emerges, his eyes terrible. He cannot say anything. But when her mother is not looking, he twists her fingers behind her back and crushes them together. 'You will pay for this.'

She pays for it. She pays and pays and pays. This has to stop. Now she declares war.

She will poison him to death. But he is a hard man to kill.

She adds urine to his food, and he does not flinch; she collects scoops of her stool and mashes it into his portion of the meal. He eats thoughtfully, chewing longer than usual, but when asked, says: Hmmm! Delicious.

She collects spiders and stirs them into his stew, and watches as he eats them.

'Can you die by eating poisonous spiders?' she asks Nouf.

'Of course.'

146

Her uncle eats dirt, snot, cockroaches and even a rotten portion of a dead rat in his chicken Biryani. But he never notices. Never weakens. Never dies.

His visits become more insistent, more perverse, more demanding of things she has to do. As if he is playing the endgame. She is becoming a woman. His desperation shows. As does her determination. Later she will have to describe these acts, but at present, she can still no words for them. He reaches into her hatred and revulsion, no matter how far she withdraws into herself.

She gets the idea while Ashraf is washing up. A glass slips and shatters on the floor and he apologises, scooping up the pieces in a cloth with trembling hands. 'Keep away from the kitchen while I clean up, Miss Amina,' he says. 'You don't want a glass splinter in your foot.'

She finds a piece that has been thrown wide. 'I'll make supper tonight.'

She grinds it with pestle and mortar to glittering white powder and sprinkles it on his curry. Stirs well. You can die from eating glass, she knows. It cuts into your colon and kidneys and bleeds you to death.

Should she?

'What's for supper,' he says. 'I'm starving.'

He always blames her or her mother for his hunger. They are responsible for assuaging all his various appetites. Women are here on this earth for that purpose alone.

What's for supper? Ground glass and spiders, Uncle.

'Chicken tikka.'

Uncle smiles. 'We'll turn you into a lady yet. More, more, please.'

Her mother smiles. 'She is behaving herself.'

She watches as he eats with a red furnace mouth and

laughs and compliments the cook on the delicious food. He burps, thumps his stomach.

She imagines this stomach being ground up, the colons writhing like snakes, cut and bleeding, the agony of a slow death that night.

But no, the night is silent and all she hears as she presses her ear to his bedroom door are deep snores.

Is he invincible?

Next day she retrieves more glass from the bin, and grinds it into his breakfast. He eats well, and has never looked better. His face glows with health.

Under the sink she finds a bottle with skull and crossbones on it and the words POISON. LYSOL. Kills 99.9% of harmful bacteria.

Next to it a bottle of bleach. Colourfast.

She follows instructions, pours two tablespoons of each into a bowl and mixes them into his coffee. Adds extra sugar.

This time it works.

By mid-morning, he looks grey and holds his stomach with both hands as if he is pregnant. That afternoon, his roars shake the house. By evening, the ambulance is parked at the front door and he is carried out on a stretcher. By midnight, her mother receives a text that he is to be admitted into the hospital for a few days.

She prays and prays.

Holds her breath.

Washes out the cup and enjoys the silence of the house, her triumph glowing like a city at night.

But he returns in three days, pale, acridly suspicious. She watches him from behind her curtains.

'Food poisoning,' he tells her mother. 'They had to wash out my stomach. What did you feed me, stupid woman?'

She hears the slap of his hand against soft flesh, and she

wants to rush out with a knife and stab him.

'Where did you get the food, woman?'

'The Falafel Place at Crazy roundabout.'

'Never buy again from that restaurant,' says her uncle, punctuating his words with slaps. 'What is wrong with good home cooked food?'

'I'm so sorry.'

Amina stands between him and her mother. He grabs her wrists together, suspends her in the air. She feels her arms are going to break. He stares into her eyes.

'Now he is no better than our father.' Amina dabs her mother's cuts and presses her own bruises with a cloth.

'Shh, Amina. That was so much worse. You forget,' her mother says. 'It's how all men are. Some are just a bit better than others.'

Nouf and Amina watch Jamal's father work on his car. Jamal crouches over the engine. He pops the hood and pulls the flat metal plug out of the oil and wipes it on his pants. Stares at the mark.

'Next,' says Jamal's father, 'we have to drain the old oil and replace the filter.'

Nouf is bored, but Amina watches him with falcon eyes.

'And this is the steering fluid.'

'If there is no steering fluid?' says Amina.

'Then the steering will seize and the driver will not be able to steer the car.'

'Where is the drain for the steering fluid?

Jamal's father shows her.

'And the brake fluid? The same?'

He nods. 'For a girl, she is not bad. Not bad.'

'I'm not a girl,' says Amina. 'Show me how to drain the brake fluid.'

'You bleed the brake fluid,' says Jamal's father. 'Like so.'

Then Jamal is taught how to change a tyre.

'Let's go,' says Nouf.

'You go,' says Amina. 'I want to learn.'

Jamal's father shrugs. He has never seen a girl like this. She has an iron will to learn. 'But why?'

'I want to be a mechanic.'

He laughs and shakes his head.

She learns the names of things, where they are located in the boot, and what to do with a flat tyre. Lugnuts. Wrench. Jack. 'Let me help you.'

'No.'

'Yes.'

It takes all her body weight and all her will to unthread the lug nuts. She stands on the wrench to loosen them. Jamal rolls out the spare tyre and they change it together, Jamal's father looking on. She is not just a girl, he thinks. She can hear his thoughts and his thoughts please her.

'Make sure you tighten the lug nuts again after you put on the new tyre. Otherwise when you're at speed, the tyre might just go rolling off.'

Amina tightens them by jumping on the wrench. 'Has it ever happened to you?'

'Once I saw it. A tyre running ahead of the car, the car crashed into a post. Very bad.'

Her uncle's car sleeps in the hot afternoon. She slips the key into the lock, pops the hood, locates the brake cable, the accelerator cable and the steering fluid.

The brake fluid bleeds black onto the concrete floor. The steering fluid is green. The wrench is located under the spare tyre in the boot. The lug nuts are tight and it takes her all her might to loosen them, all four tyres, and she is sweating and dizzy, and out of breath. But happy.

That evening, she watches her uncle drive off into the city at dusk. The car sounds angry. She listens to him as far as she can until the sound melts into the sound of the city noise and he disappears into the haze of brown.

She prays. At midnight, her mother crouches by her bed. 'There's been an accident.'

'What?'

'I have to go to the hospital.'

Sunrise is bright that next day, a lifting of a veil, a gift of childhood returned. Amina's stomach fizzes with Pepsi bubbles.

Her mother returns pale.

'What happened?'

'He lost control of the car. Hit another car and drove over the Corniche into the water.'

'Is he OK?'

'He's dead.'

She presses her lips together and her mother mistakes this for grief. She buries her face in her pillow. Amina's mother shakes. She holds Amina's head. 'What are we going to do for money?'

Amina pushes open the door that has smelled of his corpse long before he died. She opens the drawer and feels for his wallet. In it she finds the stash of bank cards.

'I'm coming shopping with you today, Mum,' she says.

'Good girl. I have to get things for the funeral. You can help me. Here is a list.'

At the Centre, while her mother shops, she hunches over the ATM and slides in a dead man's card.

The password please.

His birthday? She does not know it.

A favourite food? *Glass? Spiders?*

A loved one?

Of course. She taps in a five letter word. It works.

Welcome!

She asks for 2000 Riyals. The money slides out, and the card returned. Another 1000. Another 5000. And then: *You have reached your maximum for the day. Have a nice day.*

The next card has a 10, 000 Riyal limit so she takes it all. With each card she withdraws all she can, and returns the next day to see if she can extract more. For five days, she can withdraw 10,000 from each card, but on the fifth day the bank declines any transactions. She wipes each card of her fingerprints and places it back in the wallet in the dead man's room. But she has 300,000 Riyals in her pants which she stuffs into an envelope and places on the mat inside the front door vestibule early the next morning, so that her mother will find it.

Her mother shakes Amina awake with tears in her eyes. 'Amina, a miracle! Look! Someone has shown us compassion. Look! Look!'

'Who was it?'

'Some relative, some act of kindness and charity from someone too modest to show his face. God bless him!'

'Will we be OK, then?'

'We'll be OK.'

A Day in the Life

You will need
1. 4 Beatles
2. a cello
3. a 42-piece orchestra formally attired yet wearing joke novelty outfits
4. an alarm clock
5. a piano
6. a crazy 22 year old cellist with pink cello and beehive hairdo, pointy glasses and tight mini skirt.

We had played with the Beatles before. No big deal for me. All orchestral stuff. The Mop Heads had the ideas, but George Martin ran the show, orchestrally at least, head screwed on right. In fact, he *was* the Beatles. They were just the Id; he was the Ego.

That day I arrived with the rest of the orchestra at EMI studios. I always felt important arriving with my pink cello case. As I walked in, passers-by stared. Wow. You're going in there?

I'm not vain, you know that. Sometimes this is the only acknowledgement artists get. Most of the time you feel empty. You get your name on the album cover if you're lucky, but most often that's it. You feel like a prostitute, get paid for other people's pleasure, not your own.

So me stepping across the zebra crossing and being ushered through the huge studio doors: that's the fame and pleasure I get. Me and the other 41 musicians.

We packed into that studio and set up. We had instructions to dress formally, so most people were in suits, evening dresses.

Why, I thought? We were not going on TV or performing for a live audience. But I wore my fake pearls, painted my lips, piled my hair high, wore my can-hardly-move-dress, my here-to-be-noticed high heels.

Not that I expected the Beatles to notice me. Ringo gave me the eyebrow once, and John stared through me a long time, thinking of something far more interesting than me. Paul? Well.

We warmed up, George Martin passed down the scores, and apologised for all the blanks and the shoddy scribbling. He had written them by hand.

We practised the odd arbitrary scrapings and blowings. Hmm. Rather like a movie score. Lots of glissando, vibrato, crescendo.

And then Paul, grinning like a four-year old, brought out the party tricks.

Oh boy.

'Take one each and pass them down. Choose carefully, choose wisely.'

False noses, gorilla masks, big glasses, party hats, clown masks.

OK, OK, they were messing with us. That's why the formal attire. They wanted to subvert it. Mock tradition.

'To help get us in the spirit of things,' said Ringo, donning a gorilla mask himself. I chose a big red nose, swept my hair around it. I looked so ridiculous in my compact powder mirror that I pulled a tongue, shrugged my shoulders and went with it.

And this is when Paul looked at me. Not through me. Smiled. Raised his left eyebrow twice.

Paul McCartney at twenty-four years old. I stared back. Eternity passed, the universe sang the hallelujah chorus, my body aligned with the stars.

I was interrupted, as you always are, by Lesley first violinist, who nudged me, snapped that spell into a thousand pieces.

'Hey, that's David Crosby,' she said, pointing with her chin. She wore a witch's hat, hooked nose and wart.

'Who?' I whispered. Stared at the caveman in the shadows with his arms folded.

'Crosby, Stills, Nash and Young. David Crosby.'

'Oh,' I said. Paul clowned about with vampire fangs in his mouth, all his attention on some chick in front.

'Never heard of him.'

She rolled her parrot blue eye-lined eyes.

Paul conducted the orchestra. He was a Peter Pan. What did he know? A young kid like me, with big ideas. He told us to start on the lowest note possible and gradually play to the highest we could. We did it.

John frowned. George Harrison hunched over his guitar, working out a riff that would be famous in a year's time.

George Martin played us the basic track of the song. Or songs. See, they had just mashed three completely different songs together, and we were going to be the glue that held them together.

Then John Lennon, are you listening to me, John Lennon called us all to order. 'We're going to make this a big orgasm,' he said. 'A climax. We're going to start slow and then build and then go wild.'

He began strumming and singing a song, not anything you'd think was remotely connected, and we played along with the score.

'…went into a dream.' Stop. Stop.

'OK,' said Paul, 'we need a waa waa here, OK?'

'OK.'

'I'd love to turn you on,' said Paul, looking directly at me. 'We need that in there somewhere.'

'Me too,' I said.

'What?' said Lesley.

'Nothing.'

'He's talking about drugs, Miranda,' she said.

The BBC banned the song later for that line about having a smoke and going into a dream. But this was more than taking drugs. 'It's not all about you,' she said. Or was it? I went into a dream myself, all watery at the knees, wading through a pond, my legs disappearing in the rippled reflection.

Sex and drugs and rock 'n roll are all one. The spirit, the body, the holy ghost. All one.

We hit the beat; they played our orchestra like it was a set of drums. Weird. Why didn't they just get Ringo – who was picking his nose at the back, chatting to some chick with straight black hair – to play?

The glissando crescendo rose and rose. Play wildly with passion, with desire, get into the spirit of the contradiction of wearing formal concert attire and a clown nose.

We got into it.

I got into it. I fell into it. I stared at Paul's eyes as I got into it.

How can someone do that to you, just another human being, take you outside of yourself, to heights of your emotions never ever before scaled, until you think you are going to burst?

I felt the world turn, the studio spin, like I was on drugs myself. Colours raced at me in kaleidoscope patterns of my childhood; I played, the notes like arrows zigzagging about the room, bouncing off walls, zinging into hearts. Hearts pulsing love in big red balloons around splashing and bursting over all of us.

George Martin, the intelligence in the room, said: 'think of glissando, think *Entry of the Gods into Valhalla* from Richard Wagner's opera *Das Rheingold*. Think the rising well of emotion, the way Thor beats his celestial hammer smashing it all up in a destructive climax.'

We spoke his language. He knew his shit.

We played, we slid, we glided, we pushed the instruments to their prudish limits and ascended up and up and up and up.

In the score George had blotted in marks in each bar for each instrument, so that we knew how far we should be sliding up. 'I just don't want you to reach the climax too quickly,' he said, winking.

So we took it slow, measured, built and built.

But at the final point when it would all splash out and erupt and burst... we stopped.

The final note was not ours to make.

'Dead quiet, everyone.'

Poised.

'We're going to make this as long as possible, so please hold your breath...'

I hung by a thread, my emotions dangling from a precipice into volcanic lava.

Release me.

One two three four: all four Beatles and George Martin banged on three pianos simultaneously.

The tapes went round and round recording the dying sounds. The VU meters flickered and engineers turned up the microphones louder and louder to catch the chord as it spread out into the past. Boosted up and up.

Rage, rage against the dying of the light.

That last note lasts forty two seconds, and you can hear the studio air conditioners humming at the end and my cough and a scrape of the chair as Lesley, silly girl, moved. And the engineer gave her such a frown then, but forever her motion will be immortalised on that record.

After the final note, John Lennon asked George to edit in the note he had told us about, a high pitched tone above

157

the range of human hearing; why, if we couldn't hear it, was the point?

'Art is about the invisible,' he said in his very John Lennonish way. 'You'll feel it, but you won't hear it. Like all good art.'

'But your animals will hear it,' said Ringo. 'Dogs will go crazy every time you play this song.'

John Lennon pushed his John Lennon glasses back onto his aquiline nose. 'Art is about the unseen, the ineffable, the outside. That's what music is about, the silences, the gaps, not what you actually hear and think, not the rational…'

That's what he said.

After the release, denouement, whatever you want to call it, the end, after the final release comes the ineffable invisible outside.

That's what I said.

And after that?

So then they asked us to chat amongst ourselves. Relax. Breathe out.

Paul walked by, turned and my heart flipped over.

'Never could see any other way,' he said to me, as if we were in the middle of an engrossing conversation.

'No,' I said, playing with my red nose. 'No other way.'

He pulled the nose, stretched it on the elastic. 'Nice nose,' he said. 'Very nice.'

And that was that.

That's all I needed to know. I was happy now. Forever.

We did not know they were recording us. And the chatter was looped onto the end of the song so you can hear me. I'm on the end, and you can hear my squeaking, and then Paul saying, 'Never could see any other way,' all spliced together into a collage kaleidoscope of chatter and noise.

'Thanks guys, it's a wrap.'

John stood and clapped his hands for our attention. 'The idea is, this is the last song on the album so when the needle reaches the end and goes around and around, it will be an infinite loop. You'll hear this rabble and think things have gone horribly wrong.'

Paul nodded. 'Like the mics have been left on by mistake and the listener is eavesdropping on things they shouldn't hear.'

Ringo grinned. 'Like voyeurs.'

Vinyl record players, for those who don't know, will play that crackling at the end of a record forever unless you pick up the needle at the end. Dogs will howl. You will hear me giggling at Paul's attention, hear the snap of the elastic on my red nose. Forever.

Sgt. Pepper was the most innovative experimental album to date. We felt we were part of the new, cutting edge, dizzy precipice of the wow.

'Let's hear it!' called Ringo.

I closed my eyes, cradled my pink cello and listened. The speakers, like upright coffins, were turned up full.

First, the John song with guitar and piano. I heard the news today, oh boy.

Then the alarm clock ringing, the silver clock with two bells some roadie had brought in.

Then twenty four bars of nothing.

Then a tide of emotion building and building and building and…

Boom.

Then the lingering end like electricity sparking on a wire in a San Francisco earthquake.

Then the babbling. Paul flirting with me. Me flirting back.

The loop, around and around.

The invisible squeal.

I felt everything in my body.

Ecstasy fluttered through our fingers for one brief time. I felt its wings beating as it struggled and flapped out of my grip.

And then? We gave back our masks, stood, stretched, packed our instruments in their coffins, clumped out into the grey day where traffic and fumes swallowed up everything. The music played in my head, the shimmering feelings brimmed and spilled, and yes, something lingered in my soul, but like ripples on a lake after a stone has fallen in, the echoes grew fainter and fainter until they were gone.

The Currawongs

'Stop it! Stop it!'

Arthur, Barry, Hank turn in unison, but when they see me, they laugh like cane toads. Arthur's aim is wide, but Barry's is deadly accurate. One pebble hits the tree trunk below the nest. Another whistles through branches and clatters on the bicycle shed roof.

'Wish I had my BB with me,' says Barry.

The other kids are watching. Laughing even. I am the alien here. No one else thinks it is an atrocity to kill baby birds in a nest.

'I'll report you. You can't do that. You can't. Stop it now!'

I am used to the way I can never get the words out, can never make my body do what I want with it. And who will I report to? Their parents who buy them guns and encourage them to shoot small animals? The principal who drowns his cat's kittens at birth because there are too many of them? My father who admits he burned grasshoppers with a magnifying glass when he was a child?

Hopeless.

But I cannot sit by and do nothing. A fire burns in my chest.

It is Hank's stone that hits the nest. The crowd cheers. Down it comes, tumbling through leaves, hitting a branch, overturning. Out fall two baby currawongs, all beaks and claws and flapping grey feathers. They hit the gravel path hard. The mess of sticks follows. I know what the boys will do if they get to them. One bird's wing sticks out, and blood dribbles from the other's head. I wheel across to the nest, reach over and scoop them into my handkerchief.

The boys have caught up with me.

'Spaz!' Arthur grabs for my satchel.

'Go away! Leave them alone.'

'Go away!' Barry mocks the way I speak. If they could, they would smash the birds' heads in. I have seen it before with the baby Miners.

'Cripple!'

'Sticks and stones may break my bones, but words will never harm me.'

It's childish. I don't know why I say it. It is what little kids say when they have no power. And it's not true: of course words harm you. Words have deformed me; words have crippled my life.

'Well then,' says Hank, 'we'd better use sticks and stones then.'

I clutch the satchel in one hand and push my wheelchair as fast up the dirt track from the school bicycle shed, but do not get far when a pebble hits me in the back, then another, and then one smacks me bang on the side of my head. I push hard, trying to keep the satchel and the baby birds steady on my lap.

'Gottim! Gottim!'

They do not follow. I call back: 'One day the animals will rise up against you. You'd better make friends with them now because on that day... on that day...'

Their laughter follows me all the way up the hill.

'Boys will be boys,' my father says at dinner that night. 'No, Danny, I'm not going to call Mr Johnson or Mr Walker. Sorry.' He takes a bite of steak, and I watch the blood ooze out onto his fingers. 'That's life, I'm afraid.'

'You should keep away from those boys,' adds my mother.

'Don't provoke them,' says my father.

'Aren't you eating?' My mother pushes my plate closer

162

to me. I prod the steak with my fork, dip it in gravy and re-arrange my food.

'I don't feel hungry tonight.'

The baby birds are ugly things. I feed them raw mince, which I have to steal from the fridge and roll into little worms to drop into their wide beaks. I try to bind a foot with a bandage, but the bird pecks it off immediately; I dab ointment on their wounds. They are trusting souls, unafraid of humans. They will die, I know. I have only prolonged their suffering. I make a nest for them out of an apple box, stuff it with grass and leaves and mince worms. They caw and caw for their mother. I am your mother now, I whisper. I know, I don't speak your language, but I will look after you.

Next morning, I check to see if the baby currawongs are still alive. I expect them to die. But they're fine. They caw when they see me hold out the mince worms. They flap their wings and claw my arm. I have to administer water with a dropper, for I have no idea how they drink. I talk to them and they listen, their pied grey heads cocked onto one side, their gold eyes bright. They understand, if not the words, the soothing tone of shared pain.

Every night my parents huddle in front of the TV, lights on, windows shut against the darkness. I park my wheelchair on the veranda outside and stare up at the sky, breathe in the moist night air. I can see the stars in colour, in three dimensions, and can hear them. They make faint music barely audible to the human ear. They send messages to those who will listen.

I like the silence most of all. But it is never quite silent enough, even out here in the outback. Trucks strain up hills far away, or engage their brakes down the pass. The mine clatters

163

and whines. And the television in the living room is louder than everything, a constant noise my parents use to fill the loneliness of their lives. They don't like me sitting outside.

'Come inside, Danny, what are you doing out there? You'll be eaten by mozzies.'

'Your favourite program is on TV.'

'Such a strange lad.'

I've had them for eight days now. They grow a lot. Still very downy on the underside. They are always hungry and I feed them crickets and worms when I can find them, and of course, mince rolled into snake shapes when I cannot. They leap onto my hand and flap their untested wings. They need to learn to fly, but I do not know how to teach them.

On the road outside my house, three boys are squashing cane toads. They have collected an apple box full of them, and as they release them, the boy with the heavy boots leaps and stamps onto them, to the cheers of the others.

I push out to see twelve dead toads on the road. 'Stop that!'

The boys pause, and when they see it is me, they release another toad and leap onto it.

'Stop!'

'They're invasive pests,' calls out John Turkington. 'My dad says whenever you see a cane toad, you have to kill it. They destroy the environment. Didn't you know that?'

'Stop it. They can't help being cane toads.'

John Turkington laughs. 'Stamp!' he says, leering into my face. 'They need to be stamped out. Stamp! Stamp! Stamp!'

The road gleams with toad blood and toad innards. Intestines and colons and sinews spread on the tarmac.

'We're the invasive pests,' I say. 'Humans are the invasive pests who destroy the environment!'

They stare.

'We need to be stamped out. Humans are the pests.'

I am surprised at what comes out of my mouth. Even here in the heat of the moment when my cheeks are red and my voice quivery, I know I am being silly. Childish. What I am saying is not logical. Yet I insist. 'We are the only animal on the planet that destroys things!' But the words come out as a stutter.

The youngest boy, at a nod from the others, pours the remainder of the toads out of the box, and in a free for all, the others squish, stamp, slide them into the tar.

'Join us, Danny,' calls John Turkington. 'It's the best fun ever!'

'He can't. Look at his feet!'

'Ride over them then.'

It is a question of finding my voice. I have never had a voice. My sentences trail off like a slug's gleaming passage on a hot concrete driveway, dry up and die. I can never finish a sentence.

Doing his best. My teachers used to write on my school reports: *struggles with articulation, expression, often frustrated and angry at himself.* A huge world inside me can never emerge. Like Dr Who's Tardis, small on the outside, and inside, a universe, a world spinning full of emotions, ambitions, yearnings, and most of all, words, sentences, long, long trails of sentences that flow endlessly out of me into the spiral entrails of galaxies. I want to be everything, everybody. I swell to burst every time I breathe. But nothing comes out. I dream too of running.

'Danny, what are you going to do about the birds?' my mother asks. 'They make such a racket all the time, and the box stinks. I'm worried they'll attract snakes.'

'Wring their bloody necks,' says my father. 'That's what I would do. They're pests. Currawongs steal eggs from other birds, you know. And they wake me up in the morning with that godawful racket. Get rid of them, Danny. Or I will.'

I am worried about leaving the birds on their own, exposed in the back garden. There are too many predators on the ground and I am afraid that one day I will return from school to find the birds dismembered and eaten by some fox or dingo. And now I have to worry about my father too. They need to be safe.

But already their instincts are at work. That afternoon, I find them leaping off the edge of the box, flapping their wings and plummeting to the ground. They return and try over and over again, cawing in triumph when they are airborne. I pile grass for them to land into to stop them hurting themselves, they are so determined. I encourage them to keep trying, acting as their ski lift every time they tumble to the ground, and muttering encouragement in the coos and caws of what I think must be bird language.

The bird with the damaged leg takes his first faltering flight. His sibling joins him. They do one circuit, then another. I whistle in encouragement, and they caw in delight at their new found power. A few more wobbly landings, a few more circuits, and they are qualified navigators of the air.

At first they can only circle my head and land in the low branches of the gumtree, but each time they go off, they fly further away. Finally they soar over the roof of the house. I expect them to disappear forever, but they return in triumph, calling loudly, hungry for their next meal. They always return. This is home, and I am their mother. How

166

long does all this take, I want to know, for currawongs to grow up.

Humans are your enemy, I tell them. Fear them! Don't trust any of them.

But I don't have to worry. Nature takes care of its own.

One morning, as the baby currawongs peck mince snakes from my hands and clamber onto my shoulder, I hear an urgent cawing.

Overhead I see two dots. Two shadows in the sky circle the house, descend with wings outstretched. Their finger feathers spread in the wind. I think of predators and shield the babies under my arms as a mother would. But then I recognise two glossy currawongs. They caw, speaking a language I now understand.

The baby birds understand too. They wriggle out of my hands and waddle out in the clearing where they can see their parents in the sky.

The two birds circle twice, calling, watching me.

And then the two babies – healed, plump, ready – leap into the air. They flap hard, squawk to their soaring parents. Take their place between them, fly higher and higher in the blue haze. I watch them become four tiny dots; listen to the echo of their distant cawing. And then they are gone.

The Khan Al-Wazir Bookshop

'Your order is ready.'

I paused. Peeked through the crack. An old man, shrouded in black, his face a shadow. 'You need to hurry. Come.'

Behind him, the concrete rubble from last night's bombing.

'I never made an order...'

He thrust the receipt in my hand. My name; the order number; the logo at the top of the yellowed paper in Arabic – *The Khan Al-Wazir Bookshop*. 'I will show you where to go.'

A sniper bullet cracked a few blocks away. He winced. 'Hurry.'

'OK.'

I wrapped myself in a grey cloak. We ducked onto the main street only for a moment, then he pulled me into an alleyway. The night's corpses, I noted, had already been collected and buried.

He crouched as he walked, occupying as little space as possible, keeping out of view as much as possible, in clothes the colour of dust. I imitated his zig-zagging path, to avoid any sniper's bead.

The crack and thump rang out as soon as we dashed across a deserted roadblock. We flattened against the concrete barrier. Someone else the target, not us, or we would be dead.

At the end of the alley, he lifted a coal bin hatch. Pointed below to a metal ladder.

'I am not going down there!'

'They're expecting you. Take the receipt.'

'Wait...'

I spoke to the grainy air.

No use standing outside like this. I clamped the receipt in my teeth, clambered down the rungs, and he lowered the hatch over my head. At the bottom, I ducked under metal piping and followed the yellow glow of light along a tight tube of tunnelling, which opened into what looked like – in the flickering candle light – a series of low rooms.

A book shop. Every available space piled high with books – on dirty shelves, in spidery coves and recesses, on the floor. And in every recess, people browsing, sampling books from shelves, turning pages, reading, pulling out volumes from shelves, placing them back, weighing them.

'Hello?'

They shrank into shadows, or turned their backs, shielded their faces with their coat-collars. I understood. You don't want to be caught reading books.

The place smelled like the past.

Weak sunlight through grey windows onto a mahogany desk. Dust worms wriggling up and down in the air. On a nearby desk an edition of Daniel Defoe's *Robinson Crusoe*. Green spine, yellow brown cover. Faded front cover. 'Is this my order?' I touched it lightly, afraid that it would fall to dust itself. Blew dust devils off it which danced into the air. I picked the book up – just to feel its substance. More like paper bark than paper; the cover looked more like a gnarled wizard's face than a picture. Heavy. Solid. Real. I sandwiched it open to the middle, brought it to my nose.

So good. It smelled of a childhood I had never had. Of ages past, when people read books for their smell, their touch, their taste. When people read books at all. And it tasted – no, I did not actually lick it with my tongue, though I was tempted to – of wet sawdust, ground wood, vanilla essence, anisole, almond, camphor, mushroom. And alcohol. Benzaldehyde. A memory of my grandfather's violin bow surged through me, that faint whiff of rosin. Mildew. Decay, the kind of decay you get in fine wine or mature cheese.

I laid it back in the dust-free rectangle on the desk, and picked up another: Enid Blyton's first novel. My heart beat faster; my head dizzied. I knew this book. *The Secret Island* of my childhood had that new smell of wood, like the Lebanon forest; and glue, like my father's workshop; but more: the smell of adventure, of excitement before we had all turned ourselves into stone. I paged through the book I had not touched for twenty years. Read old familiar magic words – *The Beginning of the Adventures; An Exciting Day; The Escape; The First Night on the Island…*

The desk was lined with books I knew. Books I loved. I passed onto another. And another. *Treasure Island*. The first *Harry Potter* book in mint condition. And here *Der Struwwelpeter*, a book I read at five years old that had haunted me all of my life. And here… on the dark shelf behind the desk, the entire series of Richmal Crompton's *William* books. My father had read these to me when I was eleven, explaining the words that were too sophisticated for me, words that promised a universe ahead.

Huckleberry Finn. Tom Sawyer.

Here waited all the old boyhood books I had lost – books I had read as a child, books I had loved, all of them new, unmarked, unblemished. On one straining shelf stood the entire Dickens collection; there an entire Shakespeare collection, a first edition of *Green Eggs and Ham*. A memory bubbled up in my mind of a childhood friend and I dyeing fried eggs with green food colouring.

The Little Engine that Could.

That was me once, before I gave up trying to get up the hill of life. And on the floor at my feet, the entire DC *Superman* collection of comics from the forties to the eighties, in tight plastic covers. Unsullied by time or boys' greasy hands. No scribbles on the back, no ripped pages.

So maybe not a second hand bookshop after all. A collector's bookshop. But what a wonderful idea. I wish I'd thought of it. I'd make a fortune. If I had only had the presence of mind to collect all the books before they vanished, and hoarded them like this. But someone had thought of it. Someone had had the presence of mind to collect, keep, store, revere, before they all disappeared. Who?

An old man – wispy white hair bundled in a turban, bushy beard, leathery face, hooked nose, gleaming eyes – stooped through a dark entrance behind the desk. He rubbed gnarled hands. More like a tree than a man.

I waved my receipt.

He nodded. 'Your book order.' He extended his branch-like hand to me. In it a large pencil with a point at one end and an eraser at the other.

'What is it?'

'Your book.' He zipped it open down the middle and loose thin pages fanned out, like pencil shavings. 'Begin anywhere.'

I held the book, and leafed through the shavings. They looked as if they would crumble.

One shaving loosened. I caught it before it spiralled to the ground. The words 'Lost Loves' headed what looked like a story.

'Read, read.'

The dim light and the grainy paper made reading difficult.

Denise sat on the desk at the Christmas Dance, watching the DJ...

I looked up. 'This is about me... The first time I fell in love.'

He motioned me to read on. I leafed further through the shavings.

Our lips touched at last, but I did not close my eyes as I should have: I stared up at the window where three grinning faces watched…

'My first kiss.'

The man gestured towards an armchair in the corner. 'Read. Read. You're safe here.' Above, through the low ceiling, I heard enemy fire.

I sat.

I leafed through the paper-bark shavings, unpeeling my past, or rather what the past should have been, because the narrative took deviations from what I remembered, offered happy endings where I remembered them being disastrous. And offered catharsis, as if I had rewritten my life just by reading it.

It wouldn't do to get these pages wet, so I wiped the tears with the back of my hand, folded the pages back inside and zipped up the book. Tucked it into my cloak pocket.

The man stood over me. 'Thank you,' I said.

'Perhaps you would be interested in this?' The man handed me a leather bound book, shoe laced together with strips of brown hand-cut string.

'*The Lost Country?*'

I knew what to expect this time, and creaked open the ancient pages as if they were the actual events themselves. A lost past, gathered up in one place and retrieved, recorded, knitted together in a story that, so unlike my life, made sense. Chapters starting with regrets turned into adventure stories where I was the hero and triumphed against all odds; mysteries, tangled as my life had been, unravelled and straightened into solutions.

'How much is this book?'

The man took the book from me, blew hard and the dust

rose and fell off it, like a flock of birds on a field. Words danced into the air.

'Stop. You can't do that.'

I caught a few words as they see-sawed around me, but like snowflakes, they melted into nothing between my fingers. The pages I touched flaked into ash.

'It's what books do,' he said.

'Who are you?

He ignored me, took a book from a shelf, slammed it on the desk, opened it in the middle. Pulled a pen from his coat pocket, as if he were drawing a sword. Without a qualm, he began writing in the book.

'Excuse me...'

'Please, please, I have to write.'

'But... this is a... it's not a blank book, not a journal. It's already... You can't write in that book...'

I watched as he wrote over the words already written.

He wasn't writing. He was moving his pen across the line of words, yes, but as he wrote, he left an empty page behind him, as if his pen sucked up the ink on the page.

'Unwriting,' he said.

'How selfish! Who else can read that book after you've been... unwriting it? No one.'

'Finished. Now yours?'

He took the pile I had placed on the desk – *Robinson Crusoe, The Secret Island* and opened then.

'Wait a minute,' he said. 'These books are blank. You've been unreading them.'

'Unreading?'

'The words are gone. Every word you read disappears. You know that?'

The beautiful *Robinson Crusoe* I had just paged through was blank where I had read passages. And as my eyes fell on words, phrases, paragraphs, they too dissipated. This now a mere journal, a blank book with feint blue lines. The small print of the copyright page still on page two – I hadn't bothered to read that but as I glanced at it, the print began to fade.

I slammed the book shut. I wondered about my pencil book now, but dared not open it.

The man pointed to a section of the bookstore I hadn't seen – through a narrow doorway. 'You'd better not go in there then.'

'Why?'

'All your possible futures are written up in those books. You don't want to unread those.'

I peered into the dark passageway.

'Whatever you do, please don't unread those books. But there are books you need at the end. And that is the only way out.'

He motioned me into the room.

I spied a book on the first shelf displayed open at page one. I could not help reading. *And then the great novel came out, the pinnacle of a career, after making all that money, fulfilling every dream, taking the courage to grab hold of every opportunity and live life to the fullest, here is the person whose words made everyone weep.*

'That's me?'

'Not anymore.'

I passed rows of books, old, dusty, but newer and newer as I reached the other end of the passage. And here were new books, freshly published, smelling of new glue and paper.

I pulled books off the shelves, saw my name emblazoned on the front cover of each. My photo on the back cover. 'Wait... these are books I've written. I don't remember writing this...'

And so many. A whole shelf of new books, tightly

packed in alphabetical order. Here, on the front – New York Times Bestseller; Millions sold. In its fiftieth print run, a classic for all time.

I pulled out one book – *The Art of Losing* – and ran my hand over the cover, smelled the new book smell.

'Is this real?'

Here was one: *The Khan Al-Wazir Bookshop*, about a character who goes into a book shop and finds a book called *The Khan Al-Wazir Bookshop* in which a character goes into a bookshop only to find himself reading a book he has written called *The Khan Al-Wazir Bookshop*.

But as I sampled it, not only the words in the book faded, but sections of the bookshelves behind me began to blacken into nothingness.

'There is the book you are after!'

I looked at the shelves, and there on the top – spied the book I wanted to read more than any other: *My Self and Other Stories*. Again, I turned to the shadow at the end of the corridor for – what was it? Permission? Or assurance – that I could do this.

He nodded. 'That is your way out.'

The shelf looked sturdy enough so, putting down the book in my hand on the table, I began climbing, placing my feet on the books on the first shelf. They held. I hoisted myself up onto the second rung of books. The shelf bowed. My fingers grasped dusty air. Only a few inches – stretch – and I touched the book. I had to stand on the third shelf, but the whole structure protested. I touched the book, grabbed at it, but the cover tore in my hand. I was desperate.

'Go on,' the man at the end of the corridor said. 'You can do it!'

I pulled the books next to it away so that it would fall closer to me but they toppled off the shelf and clattered to the floor and clouds of dust rose up. I reached, stretched, dodging the books which tumbled down.

I must have it. I must know.

The shelf began to sway and fall backwards, and the books – like teeth in a nightmare – popped out of the shelves and fell around me, hitting me in the face. I tasted hundred year old dust.

The shelf gave and the book I wanted crumpled to grey powder as I grasped it. And over I went, backwards, into a cloud of dust, bracing for impact as I hit the floor.

Too late. My body all papery, my thoughts like butterflies flittering away and melting in the air as I crumbled to hundred year old dust.

Emoticon

He contacts me after ten years, out of the big, bad blue. Googles me, finds me on Facebook, and sends me this long text about how stupid he was, how much he's thinking of me now, and shit.

'Hey, Ange,' he goes, 'it's me, Bry. It's been ten years. God!' He adds an emoticon of a shocked face with mouth open.

I do not know what to do. I leave it hanging for a day. Another day.

'Hey, Ange, I had a dream about you last night, which is why I'm contacting you after all these years.' Smiley face.

He can see when I'm online, that's the trouble. I quickly sign out of Facebook. Next time I go on: 'Angie, you there?'

Of course I'm there. The little green dot next to my name tells the whole damn world I am.

'I can understand if you don't want to speak to me. I don't want to interfere in your life.'

Bryan Hutting likes your personal Facebook page, Bryan Hutting has visited your webpage, Bryan Hutting has invited you to LinkedIn. Bryan Hutting likes your post. Bryan Hutting invites you to be his friend. Bryan Hutting is online now.

Shit.

'What are you doing with your life?

'I know you must hate me, Ange.'

I do, I do, I do, I do, I do.

Confession: ten years ago, Bryan Hutting and I had a fling, or however you want to describe six months of sleepless raw lust and passion and love. Yes, love. I fell in love with him, he rode roughshod over all my defences, my

177

irony, my steel reserve and crashed into my soul; then, when I was just getting used to his occupation, he drove his tanks out, abandoned me like a Middle Eastern city after a shelling. I was all concrete rubble. Grass grew through all the broken foundations, over all the debris, but the ruins remained.

Now he's back with bubbly sentence fragments, smiley faces, exclamation marks and emoticons. How do you respond to someone whom you have had to block out of your life brick by imaginary brick over the years?

I ask Kate, my best buddy, what I should do.

Tell him to fuck off, she says. Here, let me write it for you on your phone: *Fuck off, Bryan you bloody bastard.* Block him. Put him in your Spam folder. He's spam, Angie. Unwanted junk. Whatever you do, DON'T write back to him.

'Hi!'

'ANGIE!!! Angieangieangieangie! You wrote back!'

On Facebook we are smiley faces, not people who have screwed each other's brains out, dragged each other's names in the dirt; he is not someone I have hated with such venom that I wanted to push his little baby face into the gravel; I am not someone he has scorned with the fury of hell for being clingy and emotionally attached and for the crime of falling in love with him. Not people who have scoured each other's hearts with wire brushes. No, on Facebook we're dangling modifiers and one-word messages.

Him: 'How are you?' Smiley face.

Me: 'Happily married. You?' O-Face.

Him: 'Me too. Married with a kid.' Heart. 'Well, *was* married with a kid.' Sad face. 'Separated.' Angry face.

Me: Sorry face.

Him: 'And it's even more complicated than that.' Face with confused squiggly mouth.

178

Me: 'I'm sorry to hear.'

Him: 'Yes, well, what goes around comes around. You remember how I dumped you for Inge?'

He actually is saying it. Admitting that he took a sledgehammer to my heart.

I can take it.

I can.

I can watch it bash into me and I feel nothing.

Me: 'I have a faint memory of that. Yes.'

Him: 'Haha. Your funny!'

Me: Clown Face.

Him: 'I ran off to Lismore with her. Runaway bride.'

Me: 'I'm so happy for you.' Sarcastic smiley face.

An irony icon would be good. Irony is the distance I have travelled away from him. The brick wall I have managed to construct to keep him out. How about a brick wall icon? He can feel it, I am sure. Or maybe not. He keeps babbling as if he has just found a long, lost buddy.

Him: 'You remember Inge, don't you? We got married and we had a beautiful baby together, who is now seven.'

Me: Brick wall icon. Why do I want to know all this? Why are you telling me all this? I don't want to know about beautiful babies. Regret icon.

Him: 'You might not want to hear it, but bare with me; there is a point to all this. Bear.'

Me: 'Not a sharp point?' Irony icon.

Him: 'Yes. Sharp. She left me. She said I was impossible to live with.'

Me: I could have told you that before you twisted my heart into a piece of mangled nuclear waste that no one would go near for ten years. Erase all that. Instead: 'Really?'

Him: 'She took my baby and walked out.'

'Maybe you deserved it.' Smiley face.

'Do I detect bitterness in your tone?'

'Bitterness? Naah. And you're still not getting my irony.'

'I am, Ange! I always get your irony. I love your irony. It hurts, I am so racked by your hurt, it hurt me for ten years and two months.'

'Impressive. You have measured my pain and ache in years and months. Anyway I think racked has a w. Racked means big breasted.' Big boobs gif.

'LOL. Anyways, she was seeing another man. Some areole.' Pouting face. A-r-s-e-h-o-l-e. Not areole. Arsehole. Damn this autocorrect.

'What do you want? Sympathy?'

'No. This is an honest bearing of the soul to show you where I'm at, how I got here... baring, not bearing. How do you turn off this bloody autocorrect? I am now on my knees asking for your forgiveness.'

'Really?

'Metaphorically. I can literally get on my knees if you want.'

'Send a photo and I might believe you.' Irony icon.

Photo uploading.

And then he actually sends a photo of him kneeling on the floor. Damn. I should not be playing here so close to the flames of the past. Irony, protect me here.

'And you?' he asks.

'I'm not sending you a pic of me.'

'No, I mean how are you? How have you been? How did you manage after... you know, after I dumped you? After I made the biggest mistake of my life?'

How am I?

Should I tell him that my life is a garbage heap of mistakes and wrong way signs? If the road sign says Wrong Way, I go that way. If a sign says Do Not Enter, I enter. My life is a series of wrong turn after wrong turn. Shall I tell him I married on the rebound in the hope it would set me right? Or that I left a job in Byron Bay I didn't like and took another one in Murwillumbah which was much worse, moved to Brisbane, hated it, came back, hated it even more. Let's just say that regret and I are best buddies. Mistakes and wrong turns are my bread and butter. And now this. I keep doing things swearing this is the last time I will ever do them. And then do them again. One day, one day I will stop.

'Well,' I go, 'I've been happy. Self-sufficient. Etc.'

'So glad to hear that.'

Sure, after the first few years of suicidal depression. 'I have two kids. I'm happy. Thank you.'

'Oh wow! So you live quite close! I thought you'd moved to Hell and Gone.'

The conversation flows like an even match tennis game. Thwock, thwack. Ping, pong. One smooth reply after another. Texting allows for sentence fragments and ellipses instead of full stops. It's like speaking. But in a speaking conversation you don't have to wait a full minute for a response. Texting allows you to multitask. So I can check my mail, type up my report, go pee, heat up my kids' lunch in between comments. He has to wait for me, or I wait long minutes for him. It's my turn to text, but I don't. I wait. And then I see:

Bryan is typing.

Bryan has stopped typing. Must have erased what he has written.

Bryan is typing again.

'I was stupid to leave you. Can you forgive me?'

I've been polishing this stone heart for too many years for that. Is there a 'shake-your-head-in-incredulity icon?

'Are you OK?' he goes. 'Are you still there?'

Sigh.

I type loudly and aggressively. 'Of course. It means nothing anymore.'

'You don't think I'm an areole?'

'No. An arsehole yes, but an areole no.'

'Haha your so funny. I like it when you swear. It feels honest, like you're expressing you're anger. And you need to vent your anger on me. It will heal me. Please vent.'

Asterisk. Asterisk. Asterisk. Asterisk. Asterisk. Asterisk.

'What are those, Ange?'

'Arsehole emoticons.'

'ROFL. LOL. Super Cool.'

'() () ()'

'And those?

'Cunt emoticons.'

Lolololol

:-:-:-

'And those?'

'Prick icons.'

And then, out of the ozone-depleted blue: 'I love you, Angie.'

'What?'

'I still love you. I never stopped loving you.'

'You left me, remember?' You stomped all over my heart with your big black boots. Told me that love was enmeshment, a bad faith surrender of the self.

'I made a mistake.'

Whoa, now we are entering nuclear radiated blowing dust territory. How has he managed to prise open that clam of a heart of mine? I wait. Read over what he has written.

'You still there, Angelina?'

I notice I am gritting my teeth as I type): 'Do not comprehend.'

Long pause. Bryan is typing.

Then: 'I have regretted that day for the past ten years. I'm sooo sorry I was soooo stupid. If you love someone it doesn't go away. I can't deny what we had. I was such a fool to let you go. Only now I see, with experience, what I lost when I lost you.'

'What experience?'

He messages: 'I want to know who you are again. It's been ten years. I've lived. You've lived. You were 19. I was 23. We were kids, for fuck's sake. We're adults now.'

'Really?'

'You're still the same,' he says. 'Your Facebook photos. Your LinkedIn, your website…'

'So you've been stalking me?'

He pauses. Then posts: 'A bit. Look, this is me now.'

He posts a selfie. Blue eyes that once sucked me into a mess.

'I'm so old now, don't you think?' Fishing icon.

I sigh. 'You're still the same.'

'The same as when you loved me?' he goes.

Cursor flashes. Silence. Time passes.

He cannot sit silent for long. That much I remember about him. 'Could you like me again?' he goes. 'A little?'

Silence.

Bryan is typing. 'You loved me then. Remember. You said so.'

'I never stopped loving you,' I write.

Delete.

Rewrite.

'Of course I fucking loved you then.'

If words could gush, Bryan's words are a flood: 'Thank you. Thank you. Thank you. But now?'

I type.

Delete before sending.

Fuck it.

Rewrite. Delete.

'You still love me, Angie?' he asks.

'What do you want me to say?'

'I don't know. I want to make it up to you. Even if your married, I don't want to let another day go by without getting you're forgiveness. You're. Your. Damn autocorrect.'

Love is the ultimate self-degradation. That much I have learned. But I don't write that.

And then: 'Perhaps I can come visit you, Angie? It's only a few hours' drive to the mountains.'

I Google Bryan Hutting. I bring up the company he works for. His address. His Facebook account. I look at his wedding photos. His child on the beach playing. The blonde wife Inge in dark glasses brooding in the background.

'What do you think? Can I visit you, Angie?'

My life, as I said, is a series of bad moves. I feel as if I slipped down a back road into a parallel universe one day and never found my way back to my life. My job, my friends, my marriage. And here I am about to make another fatal navigation error. Turn around where possible.

This is wrong on so many levels. I've spent ten years eradicating him from every wrinkle in my life. 'What do you want me to do?'

'I want to repair the damage. The rejection, the spurning. Those silly games I played with your heart. I know what it feels like now.'

'What are you saying?'

'I want to heal your wounds. It's the least I can do. I own a cabin near Mt Warning. Meet me there. Then you can go back to your life, your husband, your happy marriage.'

Rows of question marks. WTF. More rows of question marks.

'I'm inviting you to my cottage in the mountains. It's not far from you. We can make up.'

'Let's get this straight: you want me to drive up there to the mountains so we can have sex as your way of saying sorry?'

'Not sex, Angie, love. There is no one like you. We don't have to make love. Just talk. I just want to see you again. I love you. You'll think about it?'

Never. I vowed for ten years never to speak to him again, never to see him again. Never ever. The last straw. I vowed never ever to fall for his tricks again. Never.

'OK.'

'OK, what?'

'I'll think about it.'

Google, should I go?

Google: as long as you don't sleep with him, you're OK.

Google, does he really still love me?

Google: Dream on, sunshine.

OK Google, take me to Wollumbin National Park, Cutters Camp.

Google: What?

I am a free human being. I'm doing this on my own terms. It's not far.

Google: OK, but you're making a big mistake. Take the Uki Road to Byrrell Creek Road. Follow for 3 kilometres. Left at Mebbin Road.

A magnificent mountain frowns at me with Old Testament judgment. But what does a steely mountain God know about broken hearts and damaged lives?

Miracle of miracles, I find my way. I arrive at the campsite, find the isolated cabin and park the car.

Google: You have arrived at your destination. Turn back when possible.

185

I sit in the car. Breathe in and out. March up to the cabin.

'Hello, stranger,' he says.

He is beautiful. He has shaved, after-shaved, dressed for a romantic evening, candles flutter behind him, aromatherapy softens the air.

He hugs me lightly showing consideration for my brittle nature. He smiles at me with a smile I always loved and tried to hate. 'Angie! Come in, come in.'

Texting is easy and smooth; talking in real life is stilted and embarrassing.

'Let me get you something to drink. Wine?'

'I don't need...'

While he's in the kitchen my phone beeps. It's him. He's texting from the next goddamn room. 'Glad you came, Angie. You don't know how much this means to me.'

'I do,' I text back. 'Glad I came too. Good to see you again, Thanks.'

'Drink?'

'OK, OK, a glass of red. Thanks.'

We are going to make love, I know it. I came all this way to find out if I still love him. Or to resolve something, I don't know. Really. Or just because I'm curious about who I was, who he was and who we are now. I hate loose ends. But I know why I came really. It's that Freudian death wish thing.

He brings two glasses of red. We clink glasses.

All is going well. I watch him stammer and grovel and justify and try to unravel reality. He is pitching for a rerun of the past, with a different outcome. We will make love, resolve everything, realise we have nothing in common and then free ourselves from each other. Or...? He reaches forward, I lean into him, and...

I see fear in his eyes. Rabbit terror. And a car driving up to the cabin. Headlights lighting up the cabin and then plunging us into darkness.

'Who?'

He leaps back.

The front door opens. She walks in.

Inge.

She dumps her keys on the table. She has not seen me in the shadows where he has pushed me. 'Bryan, you won't believe this, they cancelled the whole damn weekend.'

'Bryan, you look pale. I did text you before I left. What...?'

It is time to announce my presence. I sip the wine. Raise the glass to her in greeting.

'And who the fuck are you?'

Bryan steps forward, still caressing his glass of red. 'This is... er... what was your name again...? Angie?'

'Angie?'

The words come out of my mouth like text, detached: 'Excuse me. I was just leaving. I thought I'd left something valuable here, but I was so wrong...' I down the rest of the wine in my glass and place it on the table.

And I walk out. The words hover in the sour air, the cursor flashing, waiting for me to finish.

Crunch on the stones. Brisk getaway steps. Cold-bucket-reality. He's not divorced. Not separated. They haven't even had a disagreement.

Until now.

Raised voices. Hers: 'Who the fuck...? Are you going to tell me... your fucking lies...'

His voice, punctuating the rain, echoing over my head: 'Calm the fuck down, Inge. It's nothing. She didn't bloody leave anything here. She is nobody, NOBODY...'

Nobody. That's me.

I rev the engine. Wheels spin in mud. I drive fast enough to escape tsunamis of defeat. Google, shut up, stop smirking and just take me home.

The message lights up my phone even before I arrive back home: Angie, I'm so sorry, it's not what you think. I've told her all about you, you are my love and I've left her, told her to go, forever, even if you don't come back to me, I've left her, seeing you made me realise… Angie? I know you're there. I can see you're online. You're reading this. Please respond.

I respond. I unfriend him, I deactivate my Facebook account, delete my virtual self, all the selfies, pics, smiley faces and emoticons that constituted my sad, pathetic, pseudo virtual life. But not before copying all his messages into one document, finding Inge, and sending her all his correspondence. At the end I hesitate. I want to finish with an emoticon, something that will summarise this whole fiasco. Is there a revenge icon? A gotcha icon? I search and find the perfect one. Yes, found it. Here. Plaster it big at the end of the messages, and press send.

Sins of the Father

I Last Words

'Your father's dying, hurry.'

Normally Aunt Margaret is placid and constrained, but she pulls me into the open front door and into the back bedroom with a roughness I didn't know she had.

'He's been asking for you,' my mother says. 'Desperately. Wants to tell you something.'

I have just missed his last conscious moment. The doctor predicted this all: semi-consciousness, coma, death.

My eyes adjust to the pink light (the heavy curtains are drawn). My mother is fussing with blankets and pillows at his bedside, and Aunt Margaret sits me down at the foot of the bed. 'You're just in time.'

He is sitting up, pulling at tissues in a box. His eyes are open but he cannot see me.

My mother clutches my hand: 'Mike, Josh is here.'

His response is to grab at the tissues and wrap them tightly around his hand. He winces.

'Where's the pain, Mike?' she says.

He smiles. 'In the railway station. Listen Cath, you can go through this hole.'

'Give me the tissues, Mike, I have a bucket here you can throw them in.'

'Throw them in Africa.' He throws the tissues in the bucket with a ceremonial flick of the wrist. He must be able to see and hear. He looks straight at me. 'Where are the cigarettes?'

'I...'

He fumbles with the tissue box (my father has never smoked in his life, so this comes as bit of a surprise to us all). He pulls out a tissue and wraps it around his finger.

'A pipe!'

'You don't smoke a pipe,' I say.

'Pike?'

'Pipe.'

'Sir Peter Bancroft,' he announces. (None of us have any idea who this person is or was). I pull out my notepad and begin to write it all down.

'Josh is here, Mike, you know that? From Australia.'

He gives no sign that he knows I am in the room. 'If you can move the bed a little, like that... just so. Give me a ring will you?'

'OK,' says my aunt, nudging me as if to say, we have to humour him, go along with him.

'It rings once then you wait for a while. What's my number?' He feels for the wedding ring on his finger. 'This ring.'

'Are you comfortable now, Mike?' says my mother. 'Just let me put these pillows up a little.'

'I'm OK, Cath. It's all changed. Something different. I don't understand old age homes.'

'You're at home, Mike, not in an old age home,' says my aunt.

'Where would I have to go? Why did you leave?'

'We're here. We never took you there. You're at home.'

'Well, I'm going to Bulawayo.'

A pause. Then: 'Who's all feena? [word indistinct] Supper a little. Don't wish to.

Where do I go? Pity I didn't. Bulawayo.'

My aunt hisses at me. 'What are you writing?'

'I'm writing it all down. What he says. His last words.'

'They aren't his last words.' My mother's eyes crinkle with tears. 'Mike, you're going to be OK.'

'So that's what that was,' he says. 'I would love the world to... I never saw the pirate treasure again.'

190

'He's talking gibberish,' whispers my aunt. 'Why are you writing it all down?'

I continue writing. 'No, it makes sense. Some sort of sense.'

'Can he hear us?'

'Are you talking about breakfast?' he says. 'At least I can go on the veranda and go along.' He takes more tissues out of the box and my mother takes them from him as you would from a naughty child. 'Leave them, Mike.'

My aunt leans over him. 'He's not in pain.'

'Not in three weeks. Verily I could drop off to sleep but it's not funny; it feels like you're having thorbs.'

I write it all down, word for word, even the indistinct words as he pronounces them. It feels important to record every word. I know later I will want to remember them. Like a dream that crumbles to dust when you wake.

'The nurse is here, Mike.'

The nurse walks in, a brusque occupier of space. She has set up office in the living room with all the medication and documentation necessary. It's better not to go to hospital these days. She takes his pulse.

'The nurse,' says my mother again as he registers that someone new has entered the room. He knows she's here. That is something.

'The nurse?' he says. 'The nurse is just trying to make a quick buck. They all are, you know. I can get the job done myself. It goes in the top.' He fumbles with the tissue box. My mother tries to take it away and he whines at her, pulls it to him. 'Spullillorinan,' he says by way of explanation.

The nurse places her hand on his forehead. 'You OK, Mike?'

'Is this my pipe? I am totally confused.'

She hands him the tissue box. 'Yes, Mike.'

'Bianca, water please. He looks from milky eyes into a

space at the far end of the bed where no one is standing. 'How big is it, Josh? Very nice Cath, now sure if it's left alone.'

'What?' my aunt says.

'The asparagus.'

My aunt giggles. 'It's pure nonsense.'

But now my father is agitated and tries to raise himself in the bed, falling down as he winces with what looks like pain. 'I want to walk. I can't get any. I want, God's sake, that nurse – what's her name – doesn't she have a bit of reston?'

He sits back and points to the tissue box. Speaks calmly. 'I want two things. Nails. That's unusual. A few days is it burger? If a window was disabled there, it would make it a problem.'

Maybe she's right – it is nonsense. I cannot even understand some of the words. He's speaking another language now, the language of the liminal space between life and death.

He looks at me, hears me scribbling. I stop, look up. 'Dad?'

'What happened to the wire?' he asks me. 'Where have you been?'

'I live in Australia, Dad. I came over. Just arrived this morning from Singapore.'

He turns to the nurse. 'A bit of water, for God's sake.'

My mother motions for a glass of water at the bedside but the nurse restrains her. Instead, she dabs his lips with a sponge. He sucks at it in desperation. 'We can't give him too much.'

I never ask why. Apparently it is bad for him. My mother's tears run down her cheek. He leans back, content. 'Poor old Josh, you comfortable there?'

'Yes, fine, Dad.'

'Am I misseening? I've done it. Where are my glasses? I'm sorry to give you this, Josh. He will be responsible to you to do washing. I mean it's like that for me. Is it still on the enu? Very dangerous compared, see?'

I am afraid I'm writing gibberish now, that all we are hearing are echoes of a life, of meaning now shattered by cancer. But then:

'Is that gun hill?'

Gunhill is a brand of cigarette, but also a suburb in Harare, Zimbabwe, where he lived for fifty years. Gunhill echoes uncomfortably in my mind, but I cannot think why.

'The first thing I want to do is get up the hill. I have to get out of this bed. Are you going to crown the squeen? Shame.'

'There, there, Mike.'

'What I want now is a glass of pure clean refreshing water.'

Those are his last words. My pen is poised for more, but he does not speak again. His eyes do not close but he sinks deeper into himself and lets the tissue box go. His hand slackens.

I type out his words, juggle them around, try to make sense of them. They look like wisps of habit, fragments of realities severed from meaning, or a private meaning where everything is a metaphor for something else that we have no access to. Other people's dreams are nonsense to us, and often to them too. But I still believe in a code and for some reason I feel I need to break this one.

Why Bulawayo, a town in Zimbabwe we have never lived or visited?

Why a pipe? Why cigarettes? He who never smoked. Why would he fumble and worry over smoking? Was his throat dry?

193

And the name Sir Peter Bancroft. Surely that is a clue? But I search on the internet and find nothing. There is no one of that name.

And the ring. He has taken to wearing his wedding ring only in the past few years of his life. Before, he claimed it was too claustrophobic.

But it is the phrase he used after that that sends chills down my spine. 'It rings once then you wait for a while.' He isn't talking gibberish. This is a confession I have in my hands.

But I have no way of deciphering it.

The sun broods like an Old Testament God over the steaming Norfolk Broads. It knows then, but I don't, that my father will go into a coma for three days and then die.

And then this will be lost forever.

II. Dear Son

Being dead is not all it's cracked up to be. For one I can't see. All I have are memories, and those are so bathed in nostalgia, I can't stand them. The past is drenched in emotion but I can't feel it anymore.

It's limbo. I'm here, nowhere really, waiting, but with no body, no senses, just a mind that goes on and on.

The only time I can do anything is when you think of me, when you call me into the world, then I can see – I'm pulled across the world and through your eyes when you evoke me, I'm there.

So how is Australia?

I never made it. I gave you my blessing. Go to Australia, I said, and I pictured you there. But I can see it's very different to what I imagined. But thanks. You take me everywhere. Dream of me. Keep me alive, a thin, healthy version of me, and show me through your eyes: 'Dad would love this,' you say, and I am there loving it.

Rene Descartes was right. I was a materialist all my life, denied that you survive your body, and here I am, outside it. Ridiculous, impossible, but consciousness lives on.

How? I don't know. Because without the senses, you cannot see hear touch taste smell. But you have the ghost of memories, you remember, you have the words.

Like a blind person who used to see. I can remember.

I see through your eyes, or through whoever evokes me. I share your struggles, your joys, your new land.

I try to give you signs, you know, but you don't get them.

At my funeral, I sent you a rainbow. It was so obvious. You saw it and the superstitious among you – mum, Uncle Andrew – said: 'It's a sign! Mike's trying to tell us something. But the harrumphs of Margaret and you – You! My son! – who said to yourself, no… it's just a rainbow. Sun hitting water vapour. No son, that's what a rainbow is made of, but not what a rainbow is.

A rainbow, a bird flying across your path, a red orchid blooming outside your bedroom window. Even your son got it: 'It's Granddad!' he said. 'Red is his favourite colour.' But then you with your know-all smile. It can't be, you think, you have taken on my cynicism about the after-life. I was so vehement about it.

If you would listen, I would tell you about it here. The dark spaces scientists call dark matter, dark energy. They sense that there is a force bigger than matter, that the material universe is only an expression of it. Plato was right, bless him. Descartes was right too, but not in the way you think.

But I am not here to convince you of the afterlife. No, I am here to speak to you about other things. You see, time

195

here is like space. You can stroll over to the past, to the future and linger over it as you would a painting in a gallery. And the past, our past, is where I spend a lot of time.

There is something I need you to do for me.

There is a box in the garage back in England. I left it there when I died. It's for you. Mum doesn't know about it. It would break her heart if she knew. I have kept this a secret from you and her. But now is the time. Five years after my death.

I notice I still have a hole in your heart – you can't read my letters without crying. You can't deal with death, with loss. That's a good thing. You keep me alive. When loved ones let us go, that's when we drift into deep space time and sever our connections. You're still connected.

The box is in the cold tight plastic container you sealed after the funeral. Your mother still hasn't gone anywhere near it.

Your cousin Philip is going to snoop around the garage and get rid of all my things soon. It's time, he thinks, to take possession of the garage. I can't be there any longer.

How can I tell you this?

In a dream? In signs in the sky?

You're so dense sometimes. You don't read signs.

A voice from God?

How can I talk when you only hear thunder and drumming rain?

No, I wasn't murdered. That's what most of us up here want to communicate. Some injustice, some wrong we need righted so we can move on.

No, this is something you need to resolve, not me.

It's an extraordinary story. I couldn't tell you when I was alive; I was too choked up with morphine, pain, self-pity and anger.

That's all gone now.

You did suspect me. I know that. So here is my confession.

I hope you can read the signs. I have left clues behind. I hope you can follow them.

III. Sins of the Father

I return from a cheery summer in Australia to an icy English winter in order to tidy up my mother's garage, and sort out all my father's belongings. The pain of his death is still sharp, after all these years.

I find his old school photos, his ink pen collection, the notes for a novel he never finished, his sketches of buildings and landscapes, and a tight scroll sealed in plastic, yellowed with age. Sensing this is something he didn't want my mother to see, I wait until she is back in the house before I unwrap it on the workshop bench. The rubber bands disintegrate as I touch them, but the canvas is intact. I recognise his hyper-realistic details, the subtle colours. His art still hangs in my mother's living room, Zimbabwean landscapes, houses we lived in, all in perfect geometric proportions, perspective lines still visible where he drew them in pencil. But this painting is a portrait of a woman sitting on a stool, naked, her breasts defiant, her nipples erect and her pubis covered by a modest hand. Her blonde hair covers half of her face.

No, he has not painted my mother. Yet the painting is dated ten years ago, when my parents were reunited, in love, recommitted, when he first found out that he had prostate cancer.

This woman stares out at me, unabashed, her smile skewed. Behind her a room stuffed with clues of her life-style presents itself: ornate furniture, a bird in a cage, a

197

window looking out to yellow Cassia trees in bloom. I see fear in her eyes, and her posture is poised for flight.

I am eleven years old. We live in a brick house in Harare, Zimbabwe. In the rainy season, thunderstorms rumble and darken the sky every afternoon. My father is at work, and he has left his workshop at the back of the garden unlocked. Escaping from the rain, I stumble into my father's sanctuary, a man cave where he can lose himself in making things, cutting, shaping, hammering, crafting wood. I love the smell of sawdust, the oil, the metal tools. I spend hours watching him plane, sand paper, hammer. But I have never been here alone. And the door has never been closed when we are inside the workshop. Until today when rivulets of water splash in, and I unwedge the door and slam it shut.

A poster tacked on the back of the door, a *Playboy* centrefold of a naked woman sitting on a bar stool. She licks an ice cream cone and stares at me with sly amusement. No matter where I turn, I cannot escape her eyes.

I open the door and bang it hard against the back wall so the poster is hidden in cobwebs and saw-dust.

How long has this been here? Has it been staring out all this time while I was chamfering, humming to my father's contented work? Does my mother know about it? Is it of someone he knows? No, no, no.

And where did he get this picture? In Zimbabwe, *Playboy* magazine, indeed all forms of what the government deems pornography, is banned. Even neighbouring South Africa is a dry country, with its Calvinistic white minority government that jails people for sexual offences such as possession of obscene literature and imagery. This image makes my heart fearful.

The story unravels from that discovery. In that instant, by some intuitive logic, I know it all.

My father is having an affair. *Post hoc ergo propter hoc.* I know. *Non Sequitur.* But still I know.

'Affair' is a silly word, but that's what they called extra marital liaisons then. An affair: an occurrence, an event, an important business matter. As if his life is an uneventful flat line, but here is an anomaly, a colour blip.

The phone rings mysteriously in the afternoon when my mother is still at work, and he is at home.

It only rings once.

'These bloody phones,' my father says.

He ambles into his study, closes the door, and phones his mate in Gunhill for half an hour. Or an hour. Or until my mother comes home from work. Then he clicks the phone down neatly as she walks in the door.

This is before the days of mobiles and texting and Facebook and private worlds. Telephones are shared public conveniences, like toilets. Affairs can only be conducted in hand-written letters, in motel rooms, and in furtively whispered phone conversations when spouses are at work.

Sometimes I pick up the phone to quiet breathing on the other end. I sense a presence waiting. 'Go away! Stop calling here!' I shout, and I hear a frustrated click and then the dial tone, a thrum like annoyed bees.

'Who was that?'

'Someone paying tricks.'

'It's the bloody local exchange. Or a wrong number.'

A few minutes later he is on the phone, talking in a monotone, so that even with my ear pressed to the study door, I cannot make out the words. But the tone is clear: it is sultry, ice cream-licking stuff.

The pattern develops into a daily routine. And like a dog salivating at the sound of a bell, when the phone rings once, he waits a few minutes and then makes an important call to Peter Willis, or Stan Stevens, or Mike Ferendinos. And

199

talks for hours, like the teenager I will become later.

Or he'll come back late at night, perfumed. 'I got in the way of some old duck spraying her hair with the yucky stuff,' he says. An office party. A school variety show. Sports event. All of the above.

I feel sorry for my mother. I know something she doesn't, something that will shatter her world as it has shattered mine. I have to shoulder this heavy secret all by myself – to protect her.

But then come the fights in the bedroom late at night. I wake up in my bed, my heart beating fast, and hear things children are not supposed to hear.

'Go back to your whore,' my mother goes. 'Don't bring that piece of shit into my bed.'

'You want it? Is that your problem?'

'No, it stinks.'

So she knows. She knows everything.

I hate my father now. But he is difficult to hate. He has transformed from a miserable old git into a bright cheery man. He begins to paint again, play music, sing in the shower.

One day, he asks me about a song I am listening to on the radio, he who hates pop music. 'It's Abba, dad, surely you know who Abba is?' The next day I find a single in his briefcase, that he has purchased in town – Abba's 'Hasta Manana'. I know it is not for my mother, or for me.

I expect divorce. Every day, I wait for the living-room-let's-all-sit-down-together-as-a-family-and-talk speech my friends have warned me about: 'Joshie, your father and I have decided to take a break from each other for a while. You will stay with Mum, or go with Dad to his new apartment. Or with Auntie Nellie in Bulawayo.'

But it never happens. They hold their marriage together, a broken thing, but a thing nevertheless, for my sake, for reputation's sake. My father is a respected member of society; my mother even more so. I later think: isn't a dead marriage, where each partner is dragging the corpse of the other around, far worse than divorce? But at eleven I am grateful for such deceit.

So I pretend not to know, my parents pretend not to know they know, and all is good. The affair drags on for months, years, becomes normal. My mother retreats into habits of motherhood and work; my father has many meetings to attend which keep him away at night, take him to Amsterdam on business, out of town a lot. They have steeled their hearts. But mine continues to bleed.

At thirteen I have had enough. The Affair is a monster sitting on my chest, choking me, making my nose run. Who is this woman who has wrecked our lives? I have to find out.

I look for clues. Easy as. In this small town, everyone knows everyone else's business.

He has taken up painting, music, writing: she must be an artist. He brings home silken threads on his jacket: she must have long blonde hair. He has a friend in Gunhill whom he visits for an hour or two at a time: she must live in Gunhill. The phone rings at predictable times, at her initiation: she must live with a husband and family, her immorality restrained by time and circumstance. He has become bright and philosophical, and scornful of my mother's limited intellect: she must be intellectually his equal, or more so.

She has to be everything my mother isn't.

He comes home singing Italian songs like '*Amore, Amore, Amore!*' and laughing to himself like a madman: she must be Italian.

'Mike, stop that!'

'I can sing if I want, woman. *Dagli occhi blu.*'

She has blue eyes.

It's all so elementary, my dear Watson. Elementary.

But I do not know for sure: he may be as innocent and as falsely accused as Susanna in the book of Daniel.

Then I meet her. And I know instantly – it's all true.

My father is a magician, gives shows for kids on weekends. Birthday parties, variety shows, street-carnivals. But mostly kids' birthday parties. And I traipse along as his assistant, to get free cake and Coke, most weekends. He insists I accompany him to a birthday party for a girl called Sandra Botticelli. 'I'd like you to meet her, Joshie,' he says. 'You need some friends. You can't sit here all day listening to trite music.'

He needs me to help him perform his famous sawing-a-woman-in-half trick. So I tag along, the unwilling magician's apprentice.

I remember it as a hot day, and he sweats in his red magician's shirt and bowtie long before we get to the house. When we arrive, I feel his anxiety, the significance of the moment when I am made to shake hands with the hostess and the birthday kid who looks twelve and has metal braces on her teeth. 'This is Sandra, Mrs Botticelli's daughter.' The mother's eyes scrutinise me, and the daughter, as if it is important that we like each other.

But it is not the daughter I stare at – it is the blonde, Italian, intelligent, artist mother.

HER.

She is just as I have imagined her, except for her face, which is not (as I have childishly superimposed) the Playboy model from the workshop. I know too, from my father's behaviour – his eyes averting mine, deferring to her all the time.

'Josh? This is Sandra.'

Sandra and I are a laboratory experiment, as if their relationship depends on our getting on. They leave us in awkward poses, hands draping on posts, hips skew, legs dangling and kicking floor boards. They – my father and HER – walk outside under a large Cassia tree, and I watch them through the living room window as they laugh, place familiar hands on familiar shoulders, touch elbows.

'Can't believe he's not here for his daughter's birthday party,' whispers one parent to another.

'He never is.'

They leave us alone in the room. Balloons bob. We are surrounded by tables of sickly sweet cake. Orange jelly wobbles as I tap the table with a nervous foot. A forlorn bird in a cage – a yellow budgie – ruffles its feathers.

Does she – Sandra – know too? We are both making an effort, not for ourselves, but for our respective parents.

'You want a drink?'

I nod. She passes me a fizzy red liquid in a plastic cup, which I sip in lieu of conversation.

I act polite; she acts polite, but we both redden and swallow and avert eyes. What does he want me to do, have a relationship with his mistress's daughter to legitimate his own?

No: the truth hits me like a sharp stab wound to my heart: if he leaves my mother and marries this woman, this girl will become my sister.

At least I know who The Woman is now. She's the mother of this gawky daughter. Her name? Bianca Botticelli. Frail, slightly wrinkled, sun damaged, but clear eyes, ironic, beautiful. Married to the town photographer, Paolo the Pirate, a man with a black beard and a patch over his left eye. And everyone in town knows Paolo the Pirate. He has taken on the Pirate role cheerily, and made it his trademark. Whenever you want family portraits, or passport photos, or glamour shots, or wedding extravaganzas, you go to Paolo the Pirate.

The magic show goes as planned, and I help by holding top hats out of which come rabbits, silk handkerchiefs and other Victorian paraphernalia, and Sandra watches me and my father with an eagle eye, as if she is thinking – this is the man who is destroying my family. She knows. We all know.

I stare through the crowd at the woman at the back of the room, who passes her hand through her blonde hair and steals glances at me, and rests familiar eyes on the sweating man in a red shirt who she has, must have, sexual relations with over and over again, in hidden corners of this very public community.

And if we all know, why keep up the pretence? Why not introduce themselves as the cuckolded and the cuckolder, and bring in the husband too, who must have stayed away because he also knows, and is disgusted by the whole affair?

The finale of the magic show is the sawing-a-woman-in-half trick. I assist. 'We need a volunteer from the audience?' All the kids stretch their hands in the air, but he wants an adult. Bianca Botticelli steps forward and lies down in the coffin on the table, he saws the box in half, the two boxes are then pulled apart and wheeled around the room by the magician's apprentice, and then placed together again, whereupon the lady volunteer, intact, in one piece again, is helped up by the magician's strong hand to much applause. 'Now she can lead a double life,' is my father's thread-bare punch line.

The husband, Paolo the Pirate, arrives just as the party winds down. She kisses him, and ushers him into the living room where my father hunches over his magic box. They shake hands. They are familiar, warm, because of course, they know each other. We all know Paolo the Pirate. And I notice, from one gesture, as she shrinks from him, that Bianca Botticelli is afraid of her husband. That he beats her, or at least shouts at her. She is unhappy in her marriage.

I'm cheating of course. I know this already. The rumours have been making the adult party circuit for years. Paolo the Pirate beats his wife. He keeps her locked away in the house. She is very unhappy, and never gets out to play Bridge or shop with her friends.

I am introduced to the husband too, and he squeezes my hand hard, as if he wants me to suffer for my father's sins. But there is no indication that he knows anything. She knows; her daughter knows; I know, but this man with a patch over one eye and a large grisly black beard straight out of a fairy tale knows nothing. He is proud, egotistical and bombastic, and perhaps this is why he can never conceive of his wife being unfaithful. As we leave, the daughter stares at me, wishing perhaps I could have consoled her, or at least acknowledged our shared pain.

Back home, I see my mother through my father's eyes, through his mistress's. She looks sunken and podgy and unintelligent and dry, a dead leaf still attached to the tree. And the story unravels so easily now: how my father must have grown out of love with her because she is working class, and he, a frustrated intellectual and artist, outgrew her like a skin you shed and slither away from, to grow a new one.

The woman's face haunts me now, and so does the eye-patched ogre. This affair is dangerous. If this man finds out, he'll kill my father. Beat up his wife. Come after the family. Don't the mafia wipe out whole families who have wronged them?

I watch my father. Though I have lived with him for thirteen years, I do not know him. At all. I have to retrace the steps, follow the parallel life my father has lived.

When did he meet her?

Will there be a time in the far distant future, on his death bed, perhaps, when he will confess to me and my mother, when he will tell us the whole story? Or will it go to the grave with him?

All I have are my detection skills. I have to patch the story together from the little I know. I have to use intuitive archaeology to dig, find shards of evidence, and piece together his parallel life.

Sometime around my eleventh birthday my father and the Artist-woman begin an affair. Or maybe before. Maybe this has been going on forever. Or maybe there were other women before Bianca Botticelli, and she is just one of a long string of affairs. That blonde woman in Kariba? Was she…?

At first they just flirt, but then it grows serious: he begins a double life, as does she – calling one another on the phone when neither spouse is at home, visiting galleries and going to shows, sometimes gliding past each other's lives on the street, at sports events, or supposed sports events. Sometimes I catch the pirate and my mother in conversation; once, yes, we even go to their home for dinner. My father lives in a universe that intersects with our own, an exciting universe where he can be himself, where his artistic, intellectual, and dare I say it, sexually liberated self flowers.

The relationship grows, then it vine thickens and entangles them. She wants to leave her husband for him; he wants to leave my mother for her. But what about the children, Mike? Sandra and Josh. I am the reason he doesn't split the family. He's seen enough of divorce and broken families to know better.

So they exercise restraint and continue to live in their

private universe. He goes overseas to a magic convention: she goes overseas to visit relatives. They meet in secret. He's a professional man in a small town. People talk.

And Paolo the pirate, with his beard and eye-patch looks more and more to me like Bluebeard, keeping that woman captive in his castle until my father rescues her. I begin to hate him too.

Which makes my father some kind of errant knight.

As much as I hate him for it, I can see this affair is beneficial for him. He gets a second wind in life. He's cheerful, whistles, laughs to himself in the shower. He stops wearing his wedding ring because it's too tight.

And for her too. She has found a way to escape oppression. My mother suffers, and she suffers gracefully.

The affair continues. For my crucial teen years, my father becomes a role model for infidelity. 'Play the field,' he tells me. 'Enjoy your youth. I never did. Sow your wild oats.'

Then something happens. I have no idea what. They break up. Perhaps it is getting too dangerous.

The husband has found out.

Someone is trying to blackmail them.

They quarrel.

My father won't leave his wife, and so Bianca gives him an ultimatum: leave her or leave me. Or it is the other way around? He begs her to escape Paolo the Pirate's clutches and live happily ever after in Amsterdam, but she refuses. She's not that stupid.

It reaches breaking point. Even as a gawky teenager, I have learned enough about relationships to know that they cannot remain static.

They teeter on a knife edge. He shouts at my mother, scowls at me, slams doors shut and shouts 'fuck'. The phone stops ringing. He stays home more often. And, surprise, surprise, he begins wearing his wedding ring again.

But the real reason, I suspect, stems from a political decision we have to make.

At Zimbabwe independence, an agreement is brokered at Lancaster House in the UK that whites can commute their pension out of the country unhindered up to four years after the new Mugabe government is installed. This will create stability, and prevent a brain drain.

That time has come. Four years after independence, whites face a hard choice: leave the country now with their pension in foreign exchange, and start a new life in the UK or Australia or Canada, and their pension will go with them untouched; or stay in Zimbabwe and commit to being here forever, as the Zimbabwe dollar is now losing its value rapidly and the government is closing all foreign exchange avenues of escape.

The family huddles in conference. The economy is collapsing, my father tells us. We have to go. We can make a new life for ourselves. Start again.

My mother is keen to go. Our neighbours have already upped and left, telling us we'd be 'fools to stay'.

But in so doing, my father will lose his secret relationship.

I think.

I don't know.

I imagine their last meeting. Not on the phone. In a motel somewhere. She raises her voice. He paces the room. She will not let him touch her. 'The country is collapsing,' he pleads. He means: 'I can't stay just because of a woman'. She throws tantrums, threatens to tell the world of their affair. 'How can you leave me here in this collapsing country... with him?'

Paolo the Pirate doesn't want to leave, she tells him. He has nothing but his business here, and doesn't want to be destitute back in Italy. He's trapped, and he wants to trap her here with him. 'Can't we run away together, just the two of us? Leave our families here.'

'I can't do that,' says my father.

'I'll die here with him. Without you. Without a life.'

'I'm sorry.'

So my father is spurned. He feels rejected, though he is the one who has done the rejecting.

Or maybe not. Maybe it is a grand Romeo and Juliet moment. They embrace. They make love. He makes one final request: 'I have to immortalise you in the secret of durable pigments,' he says. 'In prophetic sonnets, in the refuge of art. And this is the only immortality you and I may share, my love.'

She perches on a stool in her living room, naked, framed by the blossoming Cassia tree outside the window. 'I have to take your soul with me,' he says. She keeps glancing towards the front door, but she is liberated too by this act of defiance, of reckless action, of *l'existence que précède l'essence*. He sketches his lines of perspective, daubs paint onto the canvas, and captures her soul in a painting that he will never show to anyone, ever, until I find it five years after his death.

He leaves the country with my mother and his pension. Throws himself at the mercy of his relatives in England. I go to Australia. Sandra Botticelli goes to university in South Africa, and her mother and father sink into the mire of the Zimbabwe economy.

My father lives out the remainder of his life in a small bungalow in England; the prostate cancer spreads into his bones, and he is given one year to live. He packs his possessions into tight boxes, and dies in a haze of morphine. He makes no death bed confession.

A year after his death, I read another obituary in the paper: Paolo the Pirate (not his real name) – much loved husband and father, will be sorely missed. Faithful to the end to his family. His loving wife and daughter.

This Guy

I met this guy at a party. Danced myself to death. You know me. I bungee jump, throw myself out of planes, off cliffs, into concrete mixer relationships. It's called self-actualisation, a way of coping with all the people I am. So I sat on this stool, see, all bright eyed and bushy tailed, and gabbled to him. And this guy sat on the stool next to me, listened, amused. He liked me, and I wanted to touch him so badly, to press him hard against me, could have fucked him there and then on the living room floor with everyone watching. I could have fucked every guy in the room, I felt so good. Peace and good will to all mankind. But the party was going slower and slower and things were beginning to stretch. Their voices for instance began to slow down and then speed up and twist, like soft toffee. The air in which the sound waves were travelling was like blobs of plastic I could touch and turn around with my mind.

There were also a number of imaginary people in the room hanging around, uninvited. My ex-ex boyfriend, and my younger self, my daggy nine-year old whining, pulling on my shirt saying she wanted to go home.

'What are you on?' she said. 'What have you been taking this time?'

'Don't worry, this is the real me,' I told her. My jaw seemed to be locked though, and my eyes very sore.

'Who you talking to?' said the boy next to me. He was wearing this cap with weird insignia on it, Green River Demons, with a red eye in front. 'You are so wasted. Are you OK?' He stared into my eyes and became three gorgeous hunks.

'Let me see your cap.' I tried to grab it but he held my wrist like a handcuff. 'Don't ever touch my cap.'

'I feel really sick.'

'Good.'

'No, I mean sick. Vomit sick. What did you give me?'

'That was hours ago.'

'I feel so hot.'

'You are hot.'

'Feel my head.' His hand was like an octopus, his fingers like tentacles. 'Hey, stop it,' I said, 'your hand is sort of melting onto my head, man.'

His fingers are like spiders. Nice spiders, I mean, not creepy ones. And nice rainbow fish, nibbling at your toes fish.

'Wow,' I said. 'Wow. Do that again.'

'It's not so bad,' he said. 'People take this all the time.'

My imaginary sister just laughed at him. She had no time for my friends. 'You're a fuckhead,' she said to him.

'Shut up!' I hissed. And to the boy: 'What did you give me?'

'Millions of people take it,' he said.

'I think we need to go to my place,' he said. 'My name's Jerry, by the way.'

'Lisa...'

'Let's go.' He pulled on my arm.

'Fuck. First I have to piss, and I'm so thirsty. Get me a drink, will you?'

I pissed and pissed. Talked to myself in the loo. Which was quite normal, really. I did it even when I wasn't high. Thing is, my ex was there too in the stall, watching me with his wry, cruel smile. 'Loser,' he said.

'Get out, you prick!'

'You OK?' said the girl waiting to use the loo after me.

'If I'm not in bed by ten o'clock,' I told her, pulling up my pants, 'then I'm going home!'

It was a joke but she didn't get it. No one gets my jokes.

The test: if Nice Boy Jerry gets my joke, then I will sleep with him, OK?

I shook hands with myself. A deal.

'You're disgusting,' said my little sister.

Jerry was waiting for me by the door, his cap pulled tight over his head, like fucking Holden Caulfield. You don't know who he is? He was some dude in a book I read once that wore his cap to bed with him. I wanted to be his cap.

'Come,' said my little sister. No, not my sister – me acting like my little sister when I was nine years old. Such a brat you are, I told her. Wait until you're my age.

'OK, Holden Caulfield, let's go,' I said.

'Why do you call me that?' he said. 'Is that your boyfriend?' You mistaking me for your boyfriend?'

'No sir. My boyfriend is right here following us. Ex-boyfriend.'

He got a fright when I said that but as he could see no one near us, he figured I was pulling his leg. His middle leg. He wished.

He drove.

I was not seeing straight, but when we got to his place, I was sure he'd made a mistake. It was all white walls and sheets and screens like a hospital. A bed in the middle of the room with lights on very loud. 'Hey, I'm OK,' I told him. 'I don't need the hospital, unless you're going to operate on me, doctor.'

He laughed. 'You're funny.'

So he did get my jokes. I laughed and he laughed at me laughing and I laughed at him laughing at me. Etc. On and on. Until I needed to go pee again.

'What is this place, Holden?'

'I'll get you a drink. You get undressed.'

'You aren't the hottest guy in the room,' I said. Trouble is, my fucking sister was still there tugging at my panties, trying to put them back on. 'Let's go home,' she said. 'This place is creepy. The guy is creepy.'

'What do you know? You're only nine years old,' I said. 'But his friend is a hunk. And let me pee, will you.'

'There's only one guy here, sis.'

'Talk shit.'

The guy waited for me to piss in his filthy yellow toilet. Jesus. Then he sat me down on the bed. All naked.

Then he went down on me. No, he didn't. Sure, he buried his face in my cleft and started worrying the little nub with his tongue, even biting it, and thrusting his worm of a finger in and out, but it wasn't me. He was doing this to someone else. I lay back bored, sick, jealous. 'Hey, why don't you do that to me?' I said. 'I'm getting lonely over here.'

He looked up at me, his cap still hooding his face. Surprised to hear me speak. 'I am doing it to you.'

No, my body was far away and whatever he thought he was doing, I was numb, felt nothing. My nerve endings had taken a holiday or he was lying.

'I really have to pee,' I said, but the girl he was fingering said nothing. My words did not even move her lips at all.

'When a girl says she has to pee, she has to pee.'

It was not pretty. Not nice. But who said I was a nice girl? I couldn't hold it any longer. I peed and peed. Surprisingly, he spluttered and pulled back, wiped his face. 'Jesus,' he said. 'That's disgusting.'

'Did she have to pee too?'

Catcher ran off to the loo.

'I agree with him this time,' said my sister, her arms folded. 'That is disgusting.'

'So much for your catcher in the rye,' said my ex.

'You shut up.' I jabbed his chest but of course my finger went right through him.

Catcher returned, wiping his mouth with a towel.

214

Fastidious guy. But he wouldn't give up. He kissed the girl, thrust in a tongue, swirled it around. And as if this was permission enough, he began to writhe and insinuate that hard worm of his into her nether regions. But again he was doing this it someone else, not me. Really.

If only he had stopped the kissing, it would have been OK. It made me sick to see him carrying on like that to another woman. There was this like welling in my throat, a terrible tsunami flooding up my gullet. And he didn't even notice me. Kiss. Kiss. Tongue. Teeth even nibbling on my lips.

'I am going to throw up.' But there was no room to say the words and even if I could have they would have come out of my mouth, not hers.

And as quick as the Green River in a flash flood, I wriggled away just in time, grabbed his cap and filled it with the fruit of all my evening's digestions. I filled up the whole cap.

'Hey, no one touches my...'

Without his cap he was another person altogether. A Catcher in disguise. He was bald, he looked way older and way different to the boy at the bar. 'Who are you?' I said.

'I can't believe you blew chunks in my cap.'

He carried the cap slowly to the bathroom so as not to spill its precious cargo. Slop, slop, slop.

And then the shower. 'Get in there,' he said. 'You're a mess.'

The needles of hot water should have felt good, but again I was watching another girl shower and wished it was me. Him lathering soap over her, smoothing her breasts, her legs. My ex was going crazy with jealousy, watching them.

'Come, it's time to go,' said my sister and she pulled me out.

'I can't leave her,' I said.

'He's the catcher, remember? He'll look after her. Stop her falling.'

But leave her we did. I never saw her again. And the Catcher guy with the cap? Never saw him either. We left these two strangers in the shower, scooted out before my ex could see, and vamoosed. Me, my sister, and I.

The Absence of Theory

'Write about what?'

'Whatever comes into your head. Don't censor yourself. Just write.'

The woman in black taps a pencil on her teeth in slow rhythm. Ta, ta, ta, like a dripping tap. The man at the back squints at the notebook in front of him in disbelief, writes one word; two words. Stops. The woman with the green hair sucks on her pen.

'It's called free-writing: put down whatever comes into your head, without stopping, without lifting pen from paper. Don't stop to think, or correct, or read back. Silence the critic in your head.'

At the front of the class, the freckled woman writes frantically, whirling page after page. The woman with kiss curls scratches at her yellow notepad as if there's something underneath she's desperately trying to reach. The man too is now writing, but his pen is dragging invisible weights behind it. The woman with green hair pushes page after page out of her way as she scribbles in rhythm – tikka tikka tat, tikka tikka tat, tikka tikka tat.

The instructor paces the room, stares out of the window at the white sky, and then back at the seven white faces in the room that haven't seen the sun for six months. He has been in Milwaukee, Wisconsin for only three of those months, and his golden tan is already beginning to grey. 'Now who would like to read out what they've written?'

They're not shy: all of them want to read what they've written. And most students have written about their love life, or lack of it. *The bastard dumped me. I was such a bitch. He's a stupid fuck.* The man at the back, in spite of what looked like strenuous activity, has

217

written only one line: 'The predator stalked his prey, as was his custom.'

The freckled woman, Elizabeth, reads a long tale with too many adverbs and adjectives, tired verbs and sentence fragments, about a car accident. Fortunately she wasn't injured because it would have broken her mother's heart. What if anything should happen to my precious baby girl?

The woman in black, Alexis, reads out her lines out in a sigh: 'Where are you, Muse, when I need you? What do you think of all this? What would you do?'

The instructor turns to the window. The snow outside is banked up four to five foot high against the roadside and has turned various shades of black from the car fumes. Snow in a Wisconsin winter, he notes, doesn't melt, but is layered on top of previous snow piles, giving a fossil record of the past few months. He can see four layers of grey to black, and it's only January. He speaks to the patterns of ice.

'Peter Elbow – yes that's his name – Elbow – advocates this type of writing. Expressivism, he calls it. Censor the critic. Tap into the unconscious. Creative writing comes from the dream space in our minds.'

'I thought this was a writing workshop,' says the woman in black, Alexis.

He stumbles over his reply – sensitive to any implied criticism of his teaching. She means, why are you talking about the theory of Creative Writing, instead of letting us just write?

'In Creative Writing classes in this institution, we follow the Iowa workshop model: every week you submit a short story to the class to workshop. By the end of the semester you will produce a highly polished short story.'

'What's the Iowa workshop model?' says Alexis.

'Craft. Craft. Craft. Show and don't tell. Murder your darlings; when in doubt, cut it out; what you write about is not as important as how you write; use the third person, present tense where possible; if you mention a gun in the first paragraph, make sure someone pulls the trigger by the end…'

'I took this class to write what I like, not to be told how to write.' Alexis speaks as much to the others as to him.

He tries not to stammer. 'Freewriting is only stage one. Stage two is to invite the critic in to edit and to form, polish and rewrite. Then revise it again. And again. And again. Writing is re-writing. What you read in a successful writer's fiction is not a spontaneous first draft, but highly crafted, re-edited, reworked material. Some writers like Raymond Carver, for example, rewrote his stories over a hundred times to get them right.'

'I'm sure inspired writers don't do that,' she replies.

'What do others think?'

The others have no opinion, one way or the other. Elizabeth taps the floor with her pointed black boot, Jennifer stares at her green painted nails; Sadie chews a horn of hair that curls conveniently into her mouth.

He does not want an altercation on the first day of class, on the first day he has ever taught Creative Writing. He does not want to hear the patronising tone in his voice. He does not want to have to defend himself. But this woman, it seems, wants to make an enemy of him. He changes tack. 'Your first assignment is a short story, and I'm not interested in what you write, just how you write. How you structure it. Plan your introduction, conclusion. Follow the formula: Freytag's pyramid. Conflict, rising action, climax, falling action, denouement.' He draws the diagram on the board.

219

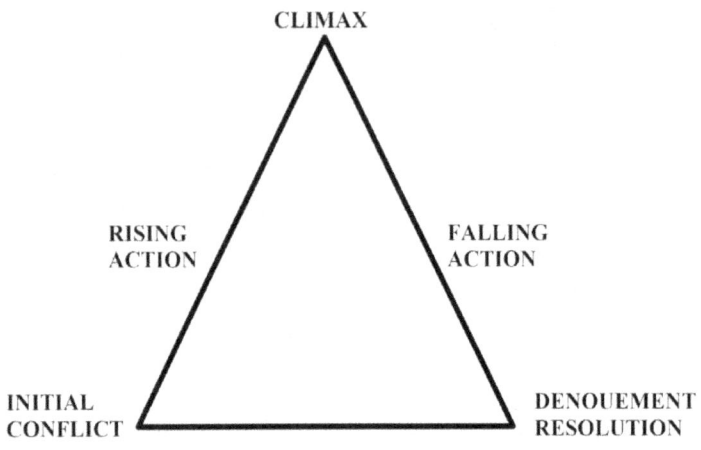

CLIMAX

RISING
ACTION

FALLING
ACTION

INITIAL
CONFLICT

DENOUEMENT
RESOLUTION

'Like sex,' Alexis says.

'Excuse me?'

She points to the diagram. 'Writing is like sex, you're saying?'

'What's the topic?' asks Jennifer.

'Anything you like. Write about your interests, your obsessions. What moves you.'

'I don't have any obsessions,' she says.

'Do you mean real obsessions, or like biting nails?'

'I have an obsession with babies,' says Elizabeth.

'My weight.'

'Go home and write about it. Whatever you like.'

Outside his office after class, Alexis is waiting. 'I have a problem.' She sits down, sweeps the black coat around her shoulders. 'I'm not sure I belong in this class.'

'Of course you do.'

She stares at him with cat-green eyes. 'I have a story I want to share, but it'll scare the shit out of the class if I read it out. And you, probably.'

'Don't restrain yourself for the sake of an audience.'

She places a cold hand on his arm. 'You're new here, aren't you?'

'I've been here three months. Flew in from Chicago on an old Turbo Prop – you know those Dash eights?'

She nods. 'You're the new hire in Creative Writing?'

He shakes his head. 'Teaching Assistant. I'm doing my PhD in Creative Writing.'

'A PhD in Creative Writing? Whatever will they think of next?'

As predicted, the stories are unformed. Never trust the first thing that comes out of your mouth, he believes, and these stories are unconscious outpourings of habit and cliché, chunks of culture undiluted. The ideas of Peter Elbow's free writing exercise the first day are supposedly to rid them of the clutter of their received ideology of culture. But all they have written is surface trivia. One is obsessed with her weight, another with her boyfriend, another with babies – not as he initially thought, the horror of having to squeeze one out of her, but with pre-packaged imagery from two hundred years of American baby kitsch – how cute they are, how she wants to steal every one she encounters just to cuddle and press against her freckled cheeks. Elizabeth has, he guesses, never had a child of her own.

The man at the back, Jan, reads a story about a predator who – predictably-kills people, five in one page, with various instruments, in melodramatic overwriting.

Alexis drums her fingers on the desk as each story is read, and flashes her green eyes at her instructor before she begins to read hers – 'The Muse'.

'Every night when the moon is up, a sassy broad applies her whore red lipstick, pulls on high boots, a short black fuck-me dress, and prowls the black streets.'

Jan stops fiddling with his pen. Elizabeth's face reddens; Sadie sucks her hair.

'But all she finds are men, men, men. She's looking for a woman. But no one has eyes, no one inspires. She returns home alone, stares up at the mirrored ceiling. At the witch's broom in the corner. At the clay statue of herself on the dresser. She watches her mirrored self as she undresses. She sips her own blood red wine, begins to seduce herself in the mirror. She bites her own arm, tastes the sharp blood, feeds off herself. Becomes her own muse...'

Elizabeth, the freckled woman, is in his office the next day, red-cheeked, and out of breath. 'Babies aren't my real obsession,' she admits. 'I didn't want to say. But after that girl...'
    'Alexis.'
    'Alexis said she was a lesbian, I thought I should come out with my real obsession.'
    'Which is?'
    'Vampires. I know it's silly, but I have these dreams every night. In the morning I can taste the blood. Like a craving. I knew what she was saying. I know it. I live it. I am a vampire.'
    He tries to discourage her. Vampires are the biggest cliché around. Number one, two and three on the best seller book lists are vampire stories. 'There's a rule in this department about genre fiction.'
    'Oh good.'
    'No, I mean you can't write genre fiction.'
    'What is genre fiction?'
    'Vampire stories. Unless you're deconstructing them.'
    'I can do that,' she says.

Next time, he suggests the class group themselves in a circle so they can read their stories aloud. The classic Creative Writing workshop. 'OK, guys, you know the rules.

The writer listens, and must not respond while the class critiques the text.'

Creative Writing workshops are based on the assumption that the text contains all the elements necessary for its comprehension. A preposterous idea, he thinks, but this is how the department operates and what the class expects, what it means by a Creative Writing class. The learning objectives call for a democratic, student centred, gender safe environment, which can all be achieved by the workshop method. In a post-structural age, he thinks, New Criticism still flourishes.

Jan presses himself against the back wall, but three bright eyed women group around Alexis at the front. They all have stories to read out about obsessions. Elizabeth begins with a poem, which she reads to the floor, her cheeks bright pink:

> *She has cast a spell on me.*
> *I am trapped inside a statue on her dressing table.*
> *I look out of green glass eyes at her, unable to move.*
>   *Who is she?*
> *She is the Lesbian-Girl.*
> *Her stomp on the world boots*
> *Her fuck-men attitude*
> *Her slow, clear, spidery voice*
> *Her whore-red lipstick*
> *She is a witch.*
> *She drives herself to madness with a silver spoon.*
> *Her broomstick in the corner of her room is sticky wet.*
> *The statue of a naked girl lies on her table, watching*
>   *her.*
> *Waiting for her.*

Alexis listens, her lips tightly pursed, her mouth freshly painted red. The class (meaning the women, for Jan is

223

silent, withdrawn) praise her, preen her, flatter her use of language, allusions, mirror references.

'That's the Eagles, right?' says Jennifer. 'Witchy Woman?'

She beams. 'You got it.'

'Is your character the same girl in Alexis's story or different?'

'Different.'

The instructor interjects. 'Elizabeth, you're not supposed to speak until the end. And you guys are not supposed to ask her questions. The author doesn't hold the key to the true meaning of the text. She has to relinquish control of her story. It's no longer hers; it's the reader's. The author is dead, or at least, has no control of the text once it's out there.'

'It is her story,' says Alexis. 'She should be able to say what it's about. And we should be able to ask her what she means.'

'OK, continue, continue.'

Green-haired Jennifer reads a story about her boyfriend. It starts badly, sentimental slush, but slowly reddens in tone, then turns purple, scarlet, black. Her voice rises in pitch as she reads, from angry to hysterical. He loved her, he used her, he abandoned her, all men are shits, she found real love with her pen pal, a girl from Utah, and when she came to visit, they kissed for the first time, and not just a kiss, but a kiss that lasted hours. 'I practised kissing myself in the mirror all my life,' she concludes. 'And suddenly I was Alice on the other side of the looking glass…'

It's self-confession, therapy, coming out of the closet. Not Creative Writing at all. He makes one last valiant attempt to intercede. 'When you say 'I' what do you mean? Who is this 'I'?'

She frowns. 'Me. Myself. Who else would it be?'

'In a story,' he explains, 'the 'I' is a first-person narrator, not to be confused with the author. Perhaps the

224

narrator, the 'I' is ironically posited. Perhaps a mouthpiece for some cultural perspective...'

Alexis interrupts. 'This is theory, isn't it?'

'What is...?'

'This 'I' and 'cultural perspective' and 'author is dead' business. Barthes. Derrida. That stuff.'

'Well, this is CR 295: The Theory and Practice of Creative Writing.'

Alexis runs her hand through her black hair. 'You want to know why I dropped the literature class? They weren't studying literature; they were studying the theory of literature, literature twice removed. And now you're telling me we're going to do theory? In a Creative Writing class?' She appeals to the class around her.

'Theory underpins everything we write,' says the instructor. 'If we don't know what that theory is, we're just victims of our own cultural assumptions.'

She speaks as if to a child who hasn't understood her the first time. 'Literary theory and creative writing have nothing to do with each other. Theory is after the fact. Creative writing is before. We're writers; it's not our business to interpret our writing.'

She pronounces the word as 'riders'. 'We riders.' 'Our riding.'

'That's also a theory. You're also espousing a theoretical perspective on what Creative Writing is, or should be...'

Alexis strides over to the window, pulls the sash up. 'It's getting way too hot in here.'

The temperature outside must be 11 Fahrenheit. The heat escapes, and an icy breath blows into the room.

After class Jan is waiting by his office door. 'I'm a bit worried about the class.'

'Oh?'

'The women are… you know… all getting together.'

'They're exploring their obsessions.'

His laugh is full of sand.

'Why don't you write about yours more? Push the envelope. See where it takes you.'

He does. Next class, it is Death with a capital D that stalks him, that won't let him go. His story is dripping with blood, with horror, with mutilation, with vengeance. His character, a Milwaukee legend, Jeffrey Dahmer, stalks his victims, dismembers them, and eats them. The victims are all young, vulnerable women, with freckles, green hair, and bright red lipstick.

'Any comments?'

Jennifer rolls her eyes quickly at Elizabeth once, but that is all the feedback Jan is going to get.

'Sadie, your story, please? Your story is called 'The Ache'?'

The woman stands on the front desk and closes her eyes. 'She is tired of being happy. In the suburbs where she lives, everyone is happy. The houses are happy, the neatly trimmed grass lawns are happy. Her mother loves her. Makes sure she is sheltered from all the nasty things in the world. They shop at malls, her mother dresses her in pretty clothes, and they live a bland, mediocre, painless, normal life…'

'Too many adjectives,' says Alexis.

Sadie's eyes are moist with tears. 'Exactly. She wants to rip off all the adjectives that smother her. Rip off the clothes her mother buys her. Rip off the smile she wears all day. Rip up all the green lawns, the sidewalks, the rows of houses, rip off the skins of her lovely neighbours. Rip off her beautiful image mirrored in the ceiling mirror she stares at every morning.'

'She wakes at midnight, sweating, and looks outside: it's not suburbs and straight lines. In her dreams, at midnight, it's... it's... writhing snakes, and bugs, all over, under the houses, in all the cracks. She sees the roads beginning to buckle and crack open – the sidewalks rolling up, uncoiling, and underneath, the wounds are red – blood oozing from every crack... a real live earth bleeding, with veins and muscles and sinews and flesh.'

Alexis taps her toe on the side of the desk in slow rhythm. The instructor notices that Jennifer is addressing her story to Alexis, and Alexis alone.

'She scratches with her fingernails. They break, the nail polish chips off, she hurts herself, but she claws and claws at the earth, desperate to find what is underneath all this... nothingness.'

She pauses, makes eye contact with the instructor, and resumes. 'But there is nothing underneath, no words, no theory, just a black space yawning, sucking. If we take away the surfaces, we are standing on nothing. Empty space, a void. She claws at her clothes, rips them off, and then her skin, then her flesh, her muscles, bones. She is trying to reach that void, that ache at the centre of her being. To get away from the words, the neat little theories of existence, the packaged explanations. A lonely ache, a pulsing as she tumbles down and around into the void. No, she screams. No.'

After a silence, where everyone, he is sure, can hear the aching thud of their own hearts, Alexis speaks. 'No theory?' she says.

'No theory.' Jennifer's eyes now avoid the instructor. And it seems they are waiting for Alexis' approval, not his. She begins to clap her hands, and the others follow. Applause. It's a performance then. They're judging this story by its raw emotion, not by its craft.

'Alexis? Your story?'

'As long as no one gets offended.'

They push the desks and chairs into a large pile at the back of the room, and hold hands in a circle. The creative writing instructor resists, but one of the students simply takes his hand and leads him to the circle. The scraping and thudding and banging brings the Literary Theory instructor from the next classroom to complain.

'"Sorry, sorry. We're doing a little experiment here."

'She locks the door against him and rejoins the circle. "Hum a single note," she says. "Then walk slowly around to the left. Now to the right, now left again." She smiles. "Keep eye contact with each other. Don't focus on the room, but on each other."

'Her green eyes command their attention. A few times around, and they stand still, but the room continues to spin around. Or the air in the room continues to whirlpool around them. They cannot stand their ground.

'"Don't look down."

'The current takes them; the room spins faster and faster.

'"It's working – don't break concentration. Go with it. Let it happen."

'They are a circle, the room is a square; now the room is a spiral, and they are pulled upwards.

'It is Rudyard Kipling's story of the tiger that ran around and around until he turned to butter. Even the instructor is melting too, into other people. He hears their thoughts, words, echoes of feelings not his own.

'The room spins and spins. Lurches into the air. It is a triumphant moment. They laugh and laugh. The room is flying. Out of the corner of his eye, she sees the campus below, and a tooth missing in the clamped jaw of the English Department building. The room bleeds bricks and splinters of wood into the grey Milwaukee air. Their hearts throb in unison, like the engine of the turbo-prop Dash 8 the instructor travelled in to get here from Chicago.

'But there is a problem. The Creative Writing instructor is tied by ropes to weights on the ground, preventing them from going higher. Cut the ropes, she says, but he refuses. We need these weights; we need the ropes. The room lurches and sways and begins to fall.

'"Hold on," she says. "Hold on."

'They pack into a hot ball, their hearts thumping in unison.

'But the room spins and jolts. With a rasp, it slots itself back in to the English Department building. But it has changed: it is slightly out of shape. The windows are larger than they were before, and the desks and chairs are rubble in the corners. Broken, splintered, useless. "Sorry," says the Creative Writing instructor. "I'm sorry".'

After class, the instructor detains Alexis briefly. She eyes him warily. 'You're upset.'

'No. You're upset. What have I done to upset you?'

'You're improving,' she says.

He turns to go, but she tugs at his sleeve. 'Why don't you share a story with us? You ask us to pour out our souls, but you don't. Don't you have a story to read to us?'

'It's not my job to foist my stories on you,' he says, flattered at this olive branch she is offering. 'My job is to help you become more conscious of your own writing processes.'

'Sad,' she says. 'Very sad.'

On Friday morning, mid-semester, a white mist rolls in from the lake, and grains the air. Inside the classroom, the light is grey. Spring is on its way.

'Julie.'

'The title of my story is called – in tribute to Jennifer's piece last week – "The Absence of Theory".'

She begins. 'I have always been ashamed of my naked body. Since my mother used to undress me in public when I was a baby, I have had this obsession, or compulsion: to hide my body from the world. Cross your legs, cover up. Never look people in the eye on the street.'

She looks up at Alexis who nods in encouragement.

'But last week I came to class naked. I don't know how it happened – I was so ashamed. I tried to hide myself from everyone, but I had nothing on. What was I thinking, to come all this way on the bus, walk through the refectory and into class naked? And as I sat down, everyone could see the cellulite in my thighs, the stretch marks on my boobs, the appendix scar – all there for people to see. Apart from my mother, no one has ever seen me naked.'

The class considers this idea. Sadie frowns. 'Ever?'

'But when I got here, what a relief to find that you were all naked too! And your bodies were like mine.'

She looks up again, at Jan. 'You were also shapeless, fat, wracked with cellulite, with pear shaped boobs.'

'Thanks a lot,' says Elizabeth.

'And Alexis…' She pauses again, but Alexis has her eyes closed, listening to the story in a faraway place.

'…began to dance us around. Like we did in your story. But this time, we were naked. I began to dance, naked, free, thinking, this is my body, broken for you. Take and eat.'

She sits down, red faced. 'The end.'

Alexis opens her eyes. Again, the class is waiting for her approval, not his. 'So there were no men in the class?' she asks.

'Only women.'

'Was this a dream you had?' asks Elizabeth. 'Sounds like a dream.'

'Or wish-fulfilment?' said Jennifer.

'It's fiction. The instructor said we could write what we liked.'

'Thank you, Julie,' says the instructor. 'And while we're on the subject of the absent men in the class, Jan has a story to read, I believe.'

Jan clears his throat, reads from his notebook. 'It's called 'Boil her flesh, crunch her bones.'

He takes her foot, and sucks on each toe – the baby toe first, then the slender three that sleep like baby children, then the big toe. She has painted them pink. She offers him her other foot, even though she's dead, has been dead for weeks now. He sucks and sucks. He swivels the foot – to his surprise, it is loose, and unscrews. He takes it off and places it in the pot of boiling water. Then her other foot. He grabs her kiss curls and holds her tight and her head too loosens, and unscrews.

Her hands are easier to detach. He sucks on each red nailed finger, and pulls them out of their sleeves. The arm comes away easily; he places it in the pot, snapping the bone at the elbow so it will fit. Her breasts are balloons with the ends dark pink nipples. They are freckled. He sucks and sucks until they deflate. He feels her soul coming through into his mouth. He savours its sweet honey taste. Now her soul is out, he can get to business. Out comes the knife, and he rips her body open from the vagina to the neck. He pulls the various parts out of her body cavity, one by one: liver, kidneys, oesophagus – sorry guys I'm not good at biology – intestines unwinding, coiled, and then finally the heart, a quivering beating thing, he holds it in his hands, and then eats it raw, while the blood drips down onto his hands and his mouth, and surprises him with its sweetness. A sweet heart, he thinks with fondness. The sweetness flows inside him, through his veins, into his own heart. He is whole again. The shaking has stopped. The deed is done.

It's outrageous, the instructor thinks. All this sucking and dismemberment, all this cannibalism and vampirism: it's all euphemism for sex. More: it's rape. Violation of those present in the class. 'Thank you, Jan. Any comments?'

At least Alexis – fiery Alexis, who blocks him at every turn, will object. And at least this story will give him the opportunity to address the problem of inappropriate allusion to persons present. But Alexis is smiling. She likes his story. 'It's about theory, isn't it? Jeffrey Dahmer is Literary theory, isn't he, and the girl is creative writing. Is that it?'

Jan hesitates. 'Yes,' he says after a pause. 'Yes it is.'

The semester spins by, and each story becomes more daring, each student pushes more boundaries, each student intrudes into the others' narrative more and more.

'For your final project, you need to polish up your stories. And – you're not going to like this, but each story must be accompanied by an expository, explanatory essay, what we call an exegesis, telling your reader on what theoretical assumptions your narrative is based, giving us your literary and theoretical contexts…'

Alexis shakes her head.

'Yes Alexis?'

'It's not my job as a writer to theorise. The creative act is mysterious and alive. You mustn't over-analyse it, unless you want it to die. Analysis presupposes a corpse.'

'How much is the exegesis worth?' ask Elizabeth. 'Could we leave it out and still pass?'

'No. It's a requirement of the course.'

'If we all leave it out?'

He sighs. 'Listen, guys, this course, the course you all signed up for is the Theory and Practice of Creative Writing. How else am I to measure your work?'

232

'Maybe we should all measure each other's work,' says Alexis. 'And measure each other by how much we have progressed. Draw a point where we started, draw a point where we arrive. By how much we have thawed, how many knots are loosened, how much we've opened up, how naked we have become.'

He considers. 'I'm open to self-assessment, and peer assessment. We can certainly discuss how we measure up to the learning objectives...'

'That's better,' says Alexis after class. 'I thought you were going to be like all the others.'

'What others?'

'The Literary Studies instructors. They talk equality, but they want conformity. To bend your will to theirs. Rape, in other words. Not mutual love making. But you...' She smiles. 'You're doing OK.'

'Thanks,' he says. 'I think.'

Elizabeth reads her final project slowly, glancing at the instructor pointedly every few sentences, to make sure he's listening.

Jeffrey Dahmer, the boy with the Raiders cap on backwards locks the door behind him, hovers over his latest victim. He eats everything; bones, flesh, sinews, gristle. Leaves the teeth. The hair gets stuck in his teeth. When the meat is digested in his gut, he gets restless. And as usual he goes on the hunt for another victim. He prowls the Cream City, finds a Creative Writing class in session. He watches from the cold outside, chooses his victim. The witch? No, too sinewy. The sweet girl buried inside herself? No. Too mushy. There that one with the green hair... yummy. Tasty. He waits for her to emerge after class, follows her home, and in the dark of a Milwaukee winter afternoon, covers her mouth with his hand, presses her against wall in a cream coloured alley. Wait! He sees with horror that his hand is smooth, not hairy. The fingernails are painted pink! Maybe it's an illusion of the dusk. He draws his knife, thrusts it into her ribs. But it is floppy and flaccid, like rubber, doesn't penetrate. The green haired girl does not scream; simply smiles at him.

He tries to pocket the knife in his jeans, and notices he is wearing a dress. He drops the knife and his hair swings into his face – he has kiss curls. He runs in terror from the girl (Wait, she calls) and at home, bolts the door and rips off the dress, hurls it in the incinerator. But to his horror, he sees that he is wearing a lace bra and pink floral panties. In the mirror, his face is smooth and freckled, and his features soft and white. His stubble has gone. He screams – a high pitched scream – when he rips off the bra and finds he has full breasts, sweating, heavy, breasts with stretch marks. He clutches his stomach – a ripping pain tears through it. When he feels down there, he has no penis. His sex is shaved, neat and pretty, a vertical line dissecting his once-scrotum. His hair is green. He has bright red lipstick. Mascara.

'Any comments?'

Jan has brooded throughout the piece, twirling his pen. But now a slow smile spreads over his face. 'It's about theory,' he says.

They have explored their obsessions, extended themselves into others, and let the cold air in. They've spun the classroom into the sky. They've fed on each other's fantasies, sucked each other's blood, cannibalised each other's body parts for use in their own stories. Jan has clawed at them, and they've clawed back at him. And they've effectively walled the instructor neatly out of their discourse. But at the end of the semester, they have to write an exegesis. They still have to be accountable.

'We have a suggestion.'

The instructor sighs. 'Okay, Alexis?'

'Seeing as you refuse to tell your story, but have to judge ours, and give us a grade, we feel that you should write the exegesis.'

'Good try, Alexis, but you have to do it.'

'Can it be a communal one?' asks Jennifer.

'Well... maybe. Collaborative learning is something the Department encourages. But it must include all your work. All seven of you.'

Alexis beams. 'OK, what form does it have to take? Objective third person, Newtonian point of view? Like: "the writer here uses Bakhtin to support her narrative strategy that all writing must be exegetic"?'

'Would you object if we wrote the exegesis in another narrative form?' Jennifer adds. 'After all, why must we as creative writers write in the dry academic style of the theorists?'

'You mean like Ficto-criticism?'

'I don't know what that is. But could we use a journal style, a personal story even, or fiction? Can we write it as a piece of creative writing?'

'That defeats the object. If you write creatively, then you'll need to explain that.'

'The critic always has to have the last word?' says Alexis. 'Is that it?'

'Yes.'

The final communal exegesis surprises him. It is a six foot square collage of their stories printed out, cut and pasted and glued on top of each other's work, in chronological order, including Jan's, in a large triangle. Each student's photo has been pasted on their work. The title 'Freytag's

Triangle' is written in spidery writing above the chart, and below and above the stories are the words 'Initial conflict', 'rising action', 'climax', 'falling action', 'Denouement'. In the centre of the triangle is a photo (taken from the Staff profiles of the university) of the instructor, behind striped prison bars. A balloon has been drawn streaming from his mouth, but it is empty. And underneath the collage is the title, taken from Jennifer's story: The Absence of Theory.

Sources

Happy Birthday Frank – winner of the *Perilous Adventures* Writing Competition, 2011

The Art of Losing – *Subtle Fiction*, 2012

The President –*Mazwi* Zimbabwe Literary Journal, published 2011

31 Murdering Creek Road – published in *Tincture* 2015

The Flat – extract from *Cokcraco*, Lacuna Publishing, 2013

Cicadas – *New Contrast*, 2012

The Magician's Son – *New Contrast*, 2005

Green Island – *Social Alternatives*, 2012

Promise me This – *Chicago Quarterly Review*, 2012, and in *Meanjin* as 'There is no Hereafter', 2013

Abstinence – *Social Alternatives* 2016

The Terrorist – extract from *Soldier Blue*, David Philip Publishers, 2008

Application for the Position of Failure – from *Fail Brilliantly*, Familius Books 2017

The Currawongs – originally published as 'Childhood' in *Social Alternatives*, 2014

Absence of Theory – *New Writing: the International Journal for the Practice and Theory of Creative Writing*, 2012

Other Books by Paul Williams

Cokcraco – A Novel in Ten Cockroaches

(2013) Paul Williams. Lacuna Publishing

Australian Timothy Turner takes up a teaching position at a university in KwaZulu, South Africa in pursuit of the reclusive and mysterious African writer, Sizwe Bantu, who is rumoured to live in the nearby misty Zululand hills. Timothy is drawn into a Machiavellian world of campus politics and suppressed desire, and must confront his own paranoia, prejudice and insecurity in search for the shocking truth.

"Without doubt the cleverest novel I've read in terms of the way it weaves narratives within narratives, around, through, under and across narratives … highly recommended to all but especially to academics, writers, teachers, literary critics and cockroaches." (*Amazon*)

Order from Amazon:

Paperback: ISBN 978-1922198-08-2
eBook: ASIN B00HQ11JUQ

Playing With Words: An Introduction to Creative Writing Craft

(2016) Paul Williams and Shelley Davidow. Palgrave Macmillan

Drawing on years of experience of writing, teaching and publishing, this book offers essential tools for writers interested in honing their craft. Whether you're a poet, non-fiction writer, novelist, journalist, student or simply a lover of words, it will take you on an exciting and challenging journey to becoming a sophisticated writer.

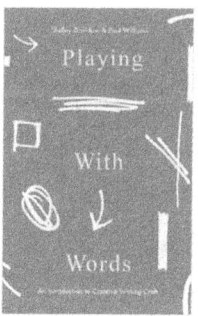

"An excellent tool kit on the art and craft of writing I will refer to again and again. Highly recommend!!!"
(*Amazon*)

Order from Amazon:

Paperback: ISBN 978-1137532-52-7
Hardback: ISBN 978-1137532-53-4
eBook: ASIN B01LZWBJ4T

Fail Brilliantly: Exploding the Myths of Failure and Success

(2017) Paul Williams and Shelley Davidow. Familius Books

Fail Brilliantly proposes a radical shift: erase the word and concept of failure from the realms of education and human endeavors. Replace it with new words and concepts. This shift in position has the potential to transform our lives and ultimately reshape our definition of success.

Order from Amazon:

Paperback: ISBN 978-1945547-25-6
eBook: ASIN B075G326X3

Other Publications by Bridge House

Keepsake

by Jenny Palmer

Keepsake and Other Stories is an anthology of short stories
by one of the growing number of brave women writers.
Jenny Palmer brings us stories of otherness, witchcraft and
magic close to home and further afield within Europe. We
meet all sorts of characters: those who rely on guard dogs,
those who shun social media and those who are obsessed.
We even meet a Neanderthal man. There are paranormal
stories, a story of bad neighbours, and a story of
redundancy. And many more. All to be enjoyed.

"Jenny is totally in control of her stories. They are memorable
and perfectly crafted." (*Amazon*)

Order from Amazon:

Paperback: ISBN 978-1-907335-57-0
eBook: ISBN 978-1-907335-58-7

Extraordinary

by Dawn Knox

From the furthest reaches of the universe, to the inside of a cardboard box, assorted characters play deadly games with their victims while others play practical jokes on angels or dirty tricks on aliens. Some have good intentions, others are scoundrels and a few are truly evil – but all of them are EXTRAORDINARY.

"A wonderful collection of amazing stories. An enjoyable read." (*Amazon*)

Order from Amazon:

Paperback: ISBN 978-1-907335-51-8
eBook: ISBN 978-1-907335-52-5

Flash Collection

Spectrum

by Christopher Bowles

A collection of one hundred and ten pieces of flash-fiction and poetry. You probably won't like all of them, and some of them might even disgust you, or make you uncomfortable. But stick with it. Look at overarching themes within each coloured block. Find the puns in certain titles. Research the colours that you've never heard of. Try and work out which stories are complete fabrications, which ones contain nuggets of truth, and which ones are versions of real life events.

"A technicolour treat – Gorgeous and provocative in all the right ways." (Amazon)

Order from Amazon:
Paperback: ISBN: 978-1-910542-13-2
eBook: 978-1-910542-14-9

Chapeltown Books